# Trouble

## J.M. DABNEY

Copyright © 2017 J.M. Dabney
Cover Art Reese Dante (Reesedante.com)
Editor: Laura McNellis

**Cover content is for illustrative purposes only. Any person depicted on the cover is a model.**

ISBN-10:1-947184-03-2
ISBN-13:978-1-947184-03-9

# DEDICATION

To the lovers of the imperfect and the ones who believe
everyone should find their happily ever after.

# AUTHOR'S NOTE

Although this is part of a series, each book can be read as a standalone. The books deal with a different couple.

Thank you for reading!

# CONTENTS

# 1 HE SHOULD'VE ESCAPED WHILE HE HAD THE CHANCE

*We don't need beer this bad!* Jimmy "Trouble" Carver gripped the steering wheel until his knuckles turned white and stared at the entrance of Granger Grocery. His friends hated him. He'd asked the cashier out on a date almost weekly for the past year, and each time, Brody turned him down.

His phone beeped beside him, he reached for it and checked the message. It was from his best friend, Landon.

Landon: *Beer! Now! - The Guys*

Why the fuck did he stay sober? If he'd drank a few beers, they wouldn't have asked him to deal with yet another humiliation. Everyone claimed he had it too easy when it came to finding a hookup. He wouldn't deny it, apart from his looks, he didn't have many redeeming qualities.

He angrily typed out a response.

Trouble: *Shut up!*

He sent the reply, shifted his hips and shoved his phone into his back pocket. They had no sympathy. What the fuck was he doing here? Because they refused to head to the store themselves. He huffed and got out then jogged toward the store. If he were lucky, Brody wouldn't be working. He slowed and walked through the automatic doors. His gaze was drawn toward the checkout lanes. Trouble nearly tripped over his feet when he saw Brody standing at his usual post at register two. Unfortunately, it seemed Brody drew the short straw today to work the afternoon lull alone.

He grabbed a cart and headed straight for the beer aisle. Picked up several twelve packs of beer, then spun toward snacks and stocked up. He slowed down and turned his cart into lane two.

"Hi, Trouble."

"Brody, how you doing?"

He unloaded the items onto the belt. Trouble barely looked at Brody. He knew what the cutie looked like. Trouble studied Brody enough to describe him in detail. Brody was short, slightly chunky and cute as fuck. Not his usual type, but the first time he'd noticed Brody he'd been helpless to resist asking him out. Only the first of many polite declines. He didn't know what Brody had against him because he'd caught the other man watching him.

"Only a few more minutes left on my shift." Each word was punctuated by a beep as Brody slid items over the scanner. "Party planning?"

"We're all at Scary's for a movie night. It's a standing tradition."

"Sounds like fun."

There seemed to be a bit of wistfulness in Brody's tone. Trouble almost opened his mouth to ask the man to join them. He couldn't take another rejection.

"We all went on our early morning ride."

Conversation wasn't exactly Trouble's strong suit and that time didn't seem to improve his skills.

Brody nodded and gave him the total. He pulled out the cash they'd pooled before he'd left.

"Daddy, Daddy," a squeaky little voice had his head popping up to see a chunky little girl with lopsided pigtails bounce up to Brody and wrap her arms around Brody's thigh.

"Honey, I told you to wait for me in the office. We're almost ready." Brody looked at him. "Sorry." The man's tanned face turned a bit pink.

"That's okay. Hi, I'm Trouble." He gave her a small wave, and the little girl hid her face against Brody's leg. She was a perfect mini-version of Brody.

"Is he in trouble, Daddy?"

The question made him bark out a loud laugh, and the color on Brody's cheeks brightened. It made Brody incredibly adorable, and Trouble wanted the man more. Trouble hadn't thought it possible.

"No, that's his name, like when I call you honey, it's a name friends and family call you."

He had to admit the two of them were the cutest duo he'd ever seen.

"Oh, hi, Trouble. I'm Mina."

"Very nice to meet you, Mina."

"My babysitter had an emergency."

3

Brody seemed to get more embarrassed by the second. He didn't understand why though. Trouble wondered where Mina's mom was. His gaze fell to the bare ring finger, but that didn't prove anything.

"Why don't the two of you—"

"We already have plans."

Hurt tightened his chest, and Trouble wanted to escape as quick as possible.

"Okay. I better get going before the boys start texting me again." He held out his hand for his change, hauled his purchases into his cart and ran as fast as he could without being too obvious.

*You're such a fucking loser, Trouble,* he muttered to himself. All he wanted to do was drive straight to his place, but since he lived with two of his friends, he would just set himself up for an extra brutal ribbing later.

♦ ♦ ♦

Three a.m. found him staring at the ceiling of Scary's living room. Landon's back to him a few feet away as his friend curled up with his partner Berserker. Lucky had his head resting on Priest's stomach as they softly snored. Scary was in his room.

Sunday nights they all crashed at Scary's even if they didn't have too much to drink; it was an unspoken rule no one drove home. He'd tried to sneak out, but Landon ambushed him and dragged Trouble back inside the house.

"You're thinking too loud," Landon whined in a sleepy voice.

"I just can't—"

In usual Landon fashion, he interrupted someone when he didn't want to wait to listen to their bullshit. "You've got to get over it."

Not everything was as easy as Landon wanted to make it. Over the past year, Landon subjected him to countless speeches.

"There's nothing to—"

"Move on."

"Quit interrupting—"

"Quit sounding like my boyfriend."

"Then shut up and let someone finish a fucking thought."

"Not if their opinion is stupid." Landon turned over and cuddled up to his side.

"Your man won't like you cuddling with other people."

"Yeah right."

To prove his point, Zerk turned over laying his arm across both of them. He shook his head, Landon giggled as Zerk's massive, hairy arm cuddled them both.

"Did you try asking him out again?"

He didn't want to talk about it, yet knew Landon wouldn't let it go. When his best friend fixated on something, Landon would see it through until the end or until someone threatened him with death.

"I invited him and his daughter to hang out, he turned me down before I finished asking."

"Daughter?"

"Yeah, cutest thing I've ever seen." He smiled in the dark. "This beautiful long curly hair and huge blue eyes. Mina was like this cute, tiny female version of Brody."

"So, you think he's straight," Landon asked.

He hated to think so because he didn't mistake the glances Brody sometimes gave him. "Probably, if I'm lucky he's bi."

"Still determined to get Brody to go out with you?"

"Maybe. I keep saying it's the last time, but I just keep setting myself up for rejection." No one could say Trouble was all that smart. They'd skipped over him when it came to brains but heaped good looks on him.

"Trouble, you've never been told no. You bat those lovely lashes, and everyone falls over themselves to do your bidding. I think it's good for you not to get your way."

"You're all heart," Trouble huffed.

"I don't think you're as pretty as you think you are."

"That's because you like grizzly bears masquerading as men."

"My man is sexy in all his hairy, husky glory."

"Whatever you say, he's not my type."

"Cute, cuddly single Daddies your type, huh?"

Trouble sighed and lifted his hands to cover his face. He didn't want to admit he hadn't had a date since Brody started turning him down. Like he didn't get enough shit from his friends already. Admitting Brody decimated his ego would be like bleeding out in a tank full of sharks. Also, no matter how hard he tried, he couldn't get Brody out of his head.

He slipped his arm between Zerk and Landon settling the smaller man's head on his shoulder.

"I'm getting too old for this shit."

"Are we having a quarter life crisis? Didn't we just celebrate your thirtieth birthday?"

Landon petted Trouble's bare chest like it was a regular occurrence. It was, none of them understood personal space. Last time they went out in a group they kept getting asked who was dating whom.

"I think I'm losing my looks."

Landon's hysterical laughter started out loud enough to wake the neighborhood before Landon slammed his hand over his mouth to stifle it.

"What's so fucking funny?"

"Jimmy *Trouble* Carver, I've known you for years, and I think you just get prettier every year. Come on, you're the tattooed, pierced, sexy bad boy that makes jockstraps fall in his wake. One man tells you no, and you go all emo like some teen goth girl who's run out of black eyeliner."

"Um, did you just compliment and insult me in the same breath?"

"Yes, maybe your cute boy has a partner at home? Probably how he got the kid."

"Brody's never—"

"Some heavily pierced and tattooed heathen called Trouble hits on you, what would a responsible—"

"Hey, I'm responsible."

"Yes, you are."

The petting resumed, and he closed his eyes. Landon was telling him what he wanted to hear to shut him up.

"You've gotta stop stressing about it."

That was easier said than done. "You're right."

"Now, keep those blue eyes closed and get some sleep. I'm frightened for your clients today."

"You're so funny, Pipsqueak."

"I know."

Trouble didn't reply and pretended to sleep. Trouble was stupid; he knew it, and his friends did too. That didn't mean the rejection didn't hurt especially when, for the first time in his life, he cared when someone said no. If someone didn't want to go out with him, he shrugged it off and moved on. He shifted to get more comfortable and cuddled Landon tighter. It was sad the closest thing to intimacy he had in close to a year was a platonic cuddle from two of his best friends. When had Trouble Carver fallen so far?

# 2 WHY DID TROUBLE HAVE TO BE SO GORGEOUS?

Brody just wanted to collapse onto his thrift store couch exhaustedly. He felt twice his twenty-three years especially when he went through all the past due notices. All he wanted to do was sleep, but Mina needed dinner, and he hadn't gone grocery shopping. He'd ignored two calls from his brother Elijah. As much as he loved his much older brother, he refused to admit defeat and accept a loan he'd never hope to repay.

His last crinkled wad of cash needed to go to pay Donna for babysitting, but as usual, an emergency came up. He needed a new sitter for Mina, but the teenager was as cheap as he found. When school started, it would be easier. He'd get off work in time to pick her up from the aftercare program offered free through the school.

His ex-wife wasn't any help. The last time he heard, she'd ended back up in rehab. He loved his daughter more than anything in life, but a weekend to himself now and again would be nice. Even the thought of it made him feel guilty.

"Daddy, I'm hungry," Mina whined from the hallway.

"Get your shoes back on, we'll go to the diner."

Mina squealed and took off running, her tiny feet pounding on the floor. He was glad he lived on the first floor because if he had a downstairs neighbor, they'd hate him. Brody dragged his feet toward the door, and just as he made it there, Mina slid into his legs. His daughter was the happiest child he'd ever met. No matter how hard things got, she lived with a perpetual smile on her face.

He opened the door, and she skipped outside. The diner was a short walk away. Besides gas money was going to be a bit tight until payday. He took her hand, and she carried on a non-stop conversation, and he inserted appropriate comments because she was ecstatic about her one-sided talk.

Fifteen minutes later, he pulled open the diner door, and the place was packed. He looked around for a free table and didn't see any. Shit, he'd said they'd eat at the diner, and he hated disappointing her. Brody never made her promises if he couldn't guarantee he could carry through.

"Brody," A familiar voice called his name, and he looked to the back to find Trouble standing, waving him over.

"Trouble," Mina yelled and took off.

"Mina," he hollered after her.

"Hey, Princess, don't you look beautiful today."

Trouble kneeled in front of his daughter as she smiled shyly. His daughter was nowhere near as shy as she pretended.

"Thank you, Trouble."

"Hey…" he waved at Trouble, "they're a bit slammed tonight."

Trouble straightened. "We've got an extra chair. Shift." He slammed his hip into a skinny guy with dreadlocks and tons of piercings.

"I like your hair." Mina walked up to the guy and started to reach out to touch his hair.

"Mina, it's not polite to touch without permission."

"It's fine, man." The stranger reached up and released his hair with thread wraps and beads intermingled throughout the thick locs.

"That's Lucky, let me introduce you to the rest of the crew. The big dude with the little spider monkey attached to him is Berserker, and the pipsqueak is Landon."

"Hi, pleased to meet you," Landon spoke up.

Brody knew a few of them from the store, but never got any of their names. Landon was slim and gorgeous, and his boyfriend was his exact opposite—huge, husky with a thick beard and barely any skin that didn't have ink or some piercing.

"The huge guy is Scary—" Trouble leaned toward him, "that's his name."

"Okay." Brody stared at the huge guy with tons of tattoos and piercings, but what made him draw back a bit was the cold look in his eyes—almost dead.

"Brody." Scary nodded.

"And the cutie beside Lucky is Priest."

"Hi, Priest. Nice to meet everyone. I don't want to interrupt." He noticed Mina missing, and he looked around to find her staring up at Scary with awe on her face.

"Why do you have earrings in your face," Mina asked, and Brody wanted to die.

"This is called an eyebrow ring, this is a septum horn which is a nose piercing, see." Scary tugged at the curved jewelry through his nose and slipped it out, then slipped it back in. "And this is a Labret which is a piercing of the lip."

"Wow!" Her eyes went wide, and Brody chuckled.

"Here, have a seat, we'll call the server over."

"I really don't want to interrupt you and your friends having dinner."

"No, it's fine, we just finished up with work and everyone but Zerk and Landon are single, so none of us cook unless threatened with starvation. Zerk or Landon take turns cooking when they're home, but we told them to come out with us instead of going back to the house to cook for the two of them." Trouble pulled out the chair beside him.

Brody hesitated yet figured what could it hurt, they were only sharing a table because the diner was busy. "It was a long day. I didn't feel like cooking. All I wanted to do is curl up on my couch, but Mina wanted food I didn't feel like making."

"She looks like she's a handful."

"Oh no, she's perfect." Brody defended his daughter, then realized Trouble smiled as he looked from him to Mina and back again.

"Where's your wife or girlfriend tonight?"

"I—I don't have either of those, it's just Mina and me." Brody watched as Mina climbed onto Scary's lap. "Mina." He called her name and earned a glare from Scary.

"She's fine," Scary growled, then looked back down at Mina.

He started showing her his tattoos, and she pushed up his sleeves to see more, tugged at the neck of his shirt.

"Will he get mad?"

"No, Scary just looks…scary. He'll answer every question she has."

Brody watched Trouble lift his arm and waved the waitress over.

"Sorry, Trouble, what can I get your friend?"

"Mina, what do you want," Trouble asked Mina.

"I want chicken nuggets and fries," she answered Trouble without looking back at him.

"Seems Scary has a new fan." The waitress giggled.

The sound odd coming from the middle age woman, but she looked around the table with a fondness he wanted to question. Trouble and his friends were a rough looking crew and a bit on the terrifying side with their height and weight. Although, he couldn't deny Trouble was downright gorgeous, with his dark blond hair and pale blue eyes. Brody wasn't as immune as he pretended, but no way could Trouble be interested in him.

"So, chicken nuggets and fries, and what can I get for you," the waitressed asked as she jotted the order onto her pad.

"Bacon cheeseburger with the works and fries. I'll take a coffee, and she'll have an apple juice if you have it."

"Great, I'll put your order in and bring your drinks right back."

"Thank you," Brody called out.

He sat there tense as Trouble laid his arm across the back of his chair. Landon and Zerk drew his attention, the two of them had their heads together and whispered to each other. They were open, even in public surrounded by strangers. They didn't hide their affection for each other.

Brody knew he was bisexual forever, but his ex-wife had been his one and only, being a single father didn't exactly leave a lot of time for dating. Also, did he want to let Mina get attached to someone who wouldn't be there for long? It's one of the reasons he never took Trouble up on his offers. The man looked like some model. Tanned, muscular, tall—fuck, what would he want with short, chunky Brody?

"How long have they been together," Brody asked and almost retreated when Trouble leaned sideways. It was disconcerting to have Trouble in his personal space. Professionalism worked as a buffer, but outside the store, it was gone.

"About a year now, but they've known each other years. Zerk works at Twirled World, Landon's parents own it."

"You're an artist?" When he asked, his gaze fell to the colorful ink gracing almost every inch of Trouble's arms. No rhyme or reason to the swirls of color interspersed with dragons which reached to the right side of his neck.

"That and a piercer, the only one on staff."

"Do you like it?"

"Nothing else I wanted to do. I practically grew up with Landon, and I became obsessed with what Gib and Peaches do. As soon as I was old enough, they took me on as an apprentice."

Trouble lit up when he talked about his work, bosses and friends. Brody had a feeling the relationship he had with the people surrounding him was more family than friends. "Landon work there too?"

"No, he's an accountant, but he takes care of the books for Gib and Peaches. They love the art, not much on the paperwork. Grow up here?"

"Yes, since I was six, my older brother moved us here after our parents died. He couldn't afford to raise me in Atlanta."

"Sorry about your parents."

Before he could say it was okay he didn't remember them, their food arrived. He started to call Mina to the chair next to him, but the waitress took her plate down the table to where Mina still perched on Scary's lap. It was weird seeing the massive man with Brody's daughter on his lap.

"Eat, Scary's got her covered." Trouble nudged Brody's plate closer.

He didn't know when he'd have another chance at an uninterrupted meal and took advantage of it. The conversation flowed around him. Some of the jokes made him blush, but when the guys got a bit too raunchy, Scary barked out an order, and it moved to safer and cleaner topics. All the while, strong fingers stroked gentle circles on his back and down his spine. He looked over to find Trouble watching him with a lopsided smile. Aside from Mina and Elijah, Brody couldn't remember the last time someone touched him for no reason. He couldn't mistake Trouble's touch for anything else but affection. Brody quickly grew confused by it.

"Why are you doing that?"

"What, touching you?"

"Yeah," Brody answered.

"Because I want to."

Trouble went silent like it was an acceptable answer. Brody glanced around the table and found everyone but Scary and Mina smiling at him. Why did he suddenly think that sitting at that table with this group of men was going to turn into a huge mistake? Hell, it wouldn't be his first and definitely not his last, but he swore he wouldn't repeat this one. The best for Mina was all that mattered and not how sexy and gorgeous he found the man beside him. That wasn't meant to be.

# 3 TROUBLE IS ON A MISSION

He pushed his fingers through his messy blond hair and opened his bedroom door. His alarm promptly went off at 11 a.m., and he tried to beat the fuck out of the snooze button for an hour. What he didn't need to see on any day, especially not without his usual pot of coffee, was Lucky's naked fuzzy ass. Which turned out to be the first thing he saw when he threw his door open.

"What the fuck are you doing," Trouble yelled through the opposite door of Lucky's room.

"What," Lucky yelled back.

"Put some fucking clothes on, you look like a starved Yeti!"

"I'm not that fucking hairy or skinny, look at these abs." Lucky motioned to his stomach. "Cut to perfection, just because yours are lost in that layer of flub."

"I'll have you know, motherfucker, there ain't a pinchable inch on this right here." Trouble patted his tight, muscled stomach.

"Are you two going to measure cocks now to see who the winner is," Zerk hollered from the end of the hall.

"No, because I'd definitely be the fucking winner," Lucky said proudly. "My abs ain't the only perfection on this manly form."

"No wonder you can't keep a boyfriend, you'd need a shoehorn to get that limp meat into the hole." He ducked a shoe that barely missed his head. "Priest, Lucky's throwing things," he bellowed as he exited his bedroom and turned left heading toward the steps.

"If you didn't provoke him, he wouldn't throw things," Priest mumbled as he shuffled out of his room. "Lucky, cover it up, I'm coming in."

"Only because it's you and I can't trust you not to become overwhelmed with lust at the sight of me."

"When are those two going to realize they're perfect for each other," he asked as he passed Zerk.

"Priest is never going to figure it out."

He knew Zerk was right. Priest spent more time in Lucky's bed than in his own, but he knew it never went passed a platonic friendship. Trouble felt sorry for the two of them, especially Lucky. A man who lived a life of complete honesty having to keep secrets had to kill him.

Trouble made it downstairs and into the kitchen. Thankfully, Landon already had the coffee going. His best friend turned to him with an annoyed expression.

"Are you antagonizing Lucky again?"

"Why is it always my fault?"

"Because it normally is."

"You had a perfectly good house, why did you move into Twirled House? Was it just to make our lives hell?" When Zerk and Landon finally got their shit together, they'd actually thought moving into the communal house was the way to go. He never claimed to associate with sane people.

"The move had to have its perks." Landon held out Trouble's bowl-sized mug. "Besides this way we can save for a house quicker."

He'd known his friends wanted to buy a house one day, and Gib rented them the place super cheap. It would definitely work for them to save up. "Not having to see Lucky's cock and balls swinging freely wasn't an incentive to stay at your old place?"

"His ass is frightening in its fuzziness."

"You agree with me."

"Drink your coffee and get ready for work."

"Yes, Dad."

He spun on his toes and headed back to his room. Trouble had more important things to worry about—Brody. It seemed things went well with Brody and Mina spending an evening with him and his friends. Mina took a liking to the crew especially Scary which was more than a little weird. He needed to get Brody to see him again, but being a single dad, dating couldn't be easy. It wasn't like he minded doing things with Brody's daughter along. The guys used the word fuck about every other word, although Scary kept the other guys in line at the diner.

Trouble slipped his phone from his pajama bottom pocket and swiped in a Z pattern on the screen. He found Brody's number which he'd gotten Brody to tell him while he was distracted during goodbyes while he kept an eye on Mina in the busy diner.

He listened to the rings and figured he'd have to leave a message the timid man wouldn't return.

"Hello," a voice not Brody's answered.

"Hey, I'm trying to reach Brody." Did the guy have a boyfriend? He'd only asked about a girlfriend or wife.

"Hold on just a second, he's getting Mina's shoes on. Can I tell him who's calling?"

"It's Trouble."

"Trouble," the stranger repeated in a suspicious voice.

"Yeah, he'll know who I am."

He walked into his room and fell back onto the bed a little too hard. Trouble held his mug slightly away from him to avoid spilling the coffee on himself. He took a sip as he listened to the muffled conversation between the stranger and Brody.

"Brody, it's some guy named—" There was a pause, and Trouble rolled his eyes. "Trouble."

"Eli, give me the phone." Brody's voice was muffled. "Hey, Trouble."

"Hi, Brody. Princess—"

"Princess?"

"We all get nicknames at the shop, she earned one."

"Oh, okay."

Brody sounded disappointed, but Trouble couldn't be sure.

"She was interested in all the ink and piercings, so I thought she'd like to see where we work."

"The tattoo shop?"

"Trouble," Princess squealed in the background. "I wanna see Trouble, Scary, Lucky, Priest, Zerk and Landon."

He felt the need to gloat about being mentioned first. They'd won over the mini-Vaughn, Trouble just needed to win over her dad. "She'll have fun and maybe y'all could join us at Twirled House for dinner. It'll probably be pizza.

We're better at making phone calls for takeout than making food."

"We?"

"Yeah, all of us, communal housing. If we're not hanging here, then we're over at Scary's place." The living situation seemed weird to outsiders. Scary's Crew at Brawlers were the same. Bull, one of the bouncers pretty much ran a halfway house for the bar's strays. Employees who didn't have a home didn't stay homeless for long. Bull could be a mean fucker, but he didn't turn anyone away.

"So, he doesn't live there?"

It took Trouble a minute to remember what they were talking about. He needed to learn to focus and not get lost in his thoughts especially when it came to Brody. Trouble didn't want Brody to think he wasn't interested.

"No, he said we're too much chaos. Makes him want to drink. What do you think? Pizza and an age appropriate movie for Princess. You'd probably have to bring the movie."

The Twirled Crew tended to lean toward gory horror movies or action ones. Except for him and Lucky, they were the only people in the house who appreciated the artistry of cartoons.

"I was going to dinner with my brother."

"He can come."

"Oh, I don't know about that."

"Come on, pizza, beer, cartoons, only after Princess starts her apprenticeship at Twirled World of course."

Trouble would damn near beg and promise anything to get Brody to spend a little more time with him. He closed in on reaching a level of pathetic he'd never seen coming.

"Okay, she's jumping up and down, repeating please."

*Score*, he mentally fist pumped.

"She'll have a great time and you will too. It'll give you a chance to relax and have some fun."

"We're going to grab some lunch, do some school shopping for Mina. We should be done around five."

"I have a one o'clock, probably put in three hours. We close for walk-ins at eight. Is that too late for dinner? We can order and have it delivered to the shop."

"That's close to Mina's bedtime."

"So, we'll eat at the shop." Trouble grasped at straws. "Okay, I gotta get ready for work. See you later, Baby."

There was a long pause, and for a moment he thought he lost the call then he heard Brody's soft okay. He disconnected the call, threw the phone on his bed and went to take a quick shower before work.

♦ ♦ ♦

Trouble's legs bounced as he kept glancing toward the door and tried to keep it as inconspicuous as possible so his asshole friends wouldn't call him on it. They already found Brody's resistance to dating him hilarious enough. He linked his fingers and cracked his knuckles. Most nights only two of them stuck around until close except for Scary who normally went to Brawlers at six to help with security.

Although tonight, Scary heard Mina was coming and decided to let his business partner Tank handle the bar. Being the boss had to have its perks. To be honest, Tank was a hell of a lot scarier than Scary. He had that whole scarred, silent dead-eyed thing going for him. No one but Scary knew the whole story of what happened to Tank, but the guy was the type to have in your corner.

He shot a look at the clock, it was coming up on six and still no sign of Brody. Maybe the man had second thoughts. Brody turned him down for almost a year. Was it possible he'd tricked himself into thinking anything about getting Brody would be easy?

"You know it was a pity yes. Now that he's come to his fucking senses he ain't coming."

"Shut the fuck up." He glared at Lucky. If the guy didn't stop talking, he'd take his ass out, and it wouldn't be the first time.

"Don't be mean because your balls are turning a lovely shade of blue. Unless your speckled STD ridden cock is still attached. I saw that last dude you brought home. I had to go to the clinic after just looking at him." Lucky shuddered and grabbed his dick as if he was warding off the specter of one of the many dick's Trouble regretted.

"My dick's just fine, motherfucker, and it's weird you're always thinking about it."

"Um, I'm gay, it's sorta what I do, reflect on the dick that is. But yours, nuh-uh, not even with the last man on Earth status. I'll get carpal tunnel and hairy palms first."

"The feeling's fucking mutual."

"I have a better chance of getting Brody bent over than you. I got personality and mad skills, you're just a beautiful face. You overcompensate with your looks for your lack of bedroom repertoire."

"You even think about his ass, and I will end you," Trouble growled as he surged to his feet, he was across the room and had Lucky in a headlock before he realized it. Lucky was laughing like a hyena.

"Guys, come on behave," Priest's exasperated tone seemed to set Lucky off more. "You're acting like idiots."

"Lucky started it," Trouble hissed through clenched teeth.

"Break it up," Scary roared.

Scary's huge hand grabbed him by the scruff and separated them.

It would almost be comical a cackling Lucky struggling against Scary's heavy hand and Trouble still trying to get at him. He froze as Scary gave them both a good shake.

"You're grown ass men, and we have company. Behave." The words were quiet enough only Lucky and he would hear them.

Trouble looked at the door to see Brody, Mina grinning as she stood in front of him and a very proper looking brunet in an expensive suit and a stern expression.

Everyone said hi at the same time.

"Scary," Mina squealed and took off for the big man.

Trouble stepped aside as his friend released them. The fact Mina took off toward his friend first hurt, but he tried not to let it get to him. Her comfort around them was critical to bringing Brody into their crew.

"Hello, Princess, don't you look beautiful today." Scary leaned down to give the tiny girl a gentle hug and then straightened.

"Thank you, Scary."

Trouble laughed at her pretend shyness as she looked way up at Scary from under the thick fringe of her dark lashes.

"Lucky, you were bad." Mina admonished Lucky even as she approached him and hugged him around his legs.

"It's a bad habit, Princess."

"Hi, Mina." He crouched down to her eye-level.

"Trouble, are you in time out?"

24

"No, we were just playing around."

Trouble let her move on to Priest, Zerk and Landon. He turned to Brody to find him shifting nervously just inside the door with the uptight dude right behind him. "Hey." He walked toward Brody and resisted the urge to draw the beautiful man into his arms. He knew deep down in his gut that Brody would run if Trouble went too fast.

"Hi, we're not interrupting, are we?"

"No, Lucky's just being Lucky." He hoped Brody didn't hear the conversation, he especially hoped Mina didn't hear it. Lucky wasn't exactly fit for the company of any age.

"Trouble, this is my brother, Elijah Vaughn."

"Mayor Vaughn?" He was related to the fucking mayor, just great. The fact the man didn't seem to like him, or the crew put Trouble getting a date near impossible.

"Yes, Eli this is Trouble."

"Hello." There was that hesitation again. "Trouble. Do you have a real name?"

"James is on my birth certificate, until I started working here everyone called me Jimmy."

"Can I—"

"No." Trouble winced at the sharp tone and smiled to soften it. "Our adoptive parents and bosses gave us the names when we started working here. We don't answer to anything else."

"O-okay."

For a politician, the guy was downright shy. It was at odds with the put-together man in front of him. "Come on, I'll introduce you to everyone. We were waiting for you to get here before we ordered pizza."

He decided to work his way from the worst one and approached Scary. "Scary, this is Mayor Elijah Vaughn,

Elijah, Scary." The silence stretched, and Trouble looked back at Elijah confused, the man's bright, almond-shaped eyes were huge. If he wasn't imagining things, it seemed like sweet, shy Elijah was checking out the massive, bad boy Scary.

"And this is Lucky." Trouble leaned in. "Don't make eye contact."

"Wow, a celebrity. Pretty too, even more beautiful than you, Trouble."

"Shut up, keep it in your pants."

"Maybe he'd love what's in my pants." Lucky sidled up to Elijah towering over the man.

Elijah froze like a prey animal. His panicked gaze darted around looking for safety. Trouble nearly choked on his tongue when Elijah took a step toward Scary. Wow, the timid man was so barking up the wrong tree there.

"Hi, pretty man, would you like to join me in the back room? I can show you I'm more than equipped—"

"Lucky, I'll destroy your fucking usefulness to all those imaginary boyfriends of yours if you don't back away now." Scary grabbed Lucky by the scruff once more.

Lucky shook off Scary's tight grip. "Fine, if you wanted to Golden Shower all over him to stake your claim, all you had to do was say so."

"I'll kill you, and no one will miss you."

"Priest would. He loves me." Lucky stated and moved away to take his usual post beside Priest.

"Th—Thank you."

"Learn to knock someone on their ass. Won't always be someone to keep someone off yours." Scary walked toward Mina. "How would you like a tattoo, Princess?"

Mina jumped straight up and down spinning until Scary carefully steered her to his chair. Seeing his friend with Mina was weird. He wouldn't have thought Scary had a gentle bone in his body.

"No—"

Trouble laughed and laid his hand on Brody's lower back. "We have washable markers. A good scrub and it'll be gone, but she'll feel like one of the crew tonight." The man looked embarrassed, so he didn't point it out. "Let the guys ink the Princess, and we'll step outside for a minute, order dinner."

"Go sit over there, Elijah, and quit staring at everyone like that it's embarrassing."

"I am not embarrassing." Elijah sent Brody a deadly stare.

Trouble led Brody outside while Elijah flopped down onto one of the couches. Again, the man's gaze on Scary. The man had to be on heavy meds.

"Will she be okay?"

"Yeah, she'll be great. All you have to do is look right through the window, and you can see her."

"Okay, sorry to be twitchy, I've only left her with less than a handful of people since she's been born."

"Everyone needs a break on occasion."

"I know." Brody sighed heavily and turned to lean back against the glass beside the door. "I wish for a break, but the thought makes me feel guilty too."

"No reason to feel guilty. You can bring her around here anytime, or by the house. Zerk has this huge dog that's like a big baby. Mina would love playing with him."

"Trouble?" Something in the way Brody said it stopped Trouble.

He turned to catch Brody watching him with an apprehensive glint in his eyes.

"Why do I make you nervous?" He closed the distance between them and placed his hands on Brody's little love handles, then took one more step.

"You're not helping me with my nervousness."

"I don't think what you feel around me has anything to do with your nerves."

Brody's breathing picked up a few notches the closer he got to Brody.

"Then what do you think it is?"

"You're attracted to me," he whispered the words against Brody's soft lips. Just that barely there contact urged him to take more. He wanted to feel every inch of Brody's sweet body against his—under his, but he needed patience, and that was something he'd never learned.

"I'm surprised you can carry around that ego of yours."

It was all bravado. Brody's pupils dilated, and Brody leaned into him. He didn't even think the man knew he was doing it.

"The shy one has some fangs. Do you know what to do with them," he asked and instantly sensed the moment Brody's timid nature came back.

"I can't have sex with you."

"Not yet." He slid his hands around the small of Brody's back and tugged him closer. The little curve of Brody's stomach conformed to his tight abs. He loved all that softness, but what would be better was having him naked and in his bed. His dick pushed against the body-warmed metal of his zipper.

Fuck, he had to stop thinking about getting his man naked.

"I can't do this."

"Why not?"

"Mina."

"I like Mina. She's a sweetheart. She gets along with the guys. She fits in good. Look." He motioned through the window to where Mina was currently the center of attention. One tiny arm was covered from wrist to shoulder with colorful ink. "More importantly, she likes it here."

Brody turned his head, and Trouble brought his eyes back to him. He took in Brody's profile, and then lower, observing the steady beat of Brody's pulse. The moment he'd set eyes on him the first time, Brody was the only man he could think about.

"She looks so happy."

"You're so beautiful." He hadn't meant to say it out loud, and Brody jerked his head around with a shocked look on his face.

"No—"

He didn't give Brody a chance to deny it. Trouble reached up, took Brody's face between his hands and finally kissed the smaller man. Tilting his head, he started to lick across Brody's lips. He groaned as Brody's mouth parted, and he began to push inside.

"Put your dick away, you're on a fucking public street," Lucky practically screamed.

"We're going to kill you." How Lucky survived to the age of twenty-eight shocked all of them.

"Why does everyone always threaten to kill me?"

"It's your fucking sparkling personality."

"I want food, and you said you'd buy. Order me food…now. Also, it's passed Priest's dinner time. He needs food. We have to be careful about his blood sugar. Dipping your dick into something pretty and tight is less important than my man eating."

"He's not your man."

Lucky huffed and turned away. "Order food," he bellowed over his shoulder.

"You're cranky when you're hungry," Trouble yelled at Lucky as the door closed.

"Is Priest Lucky's boyfriend?"

"No, best friends, but watching the two it does seem like they're a couple."

"So, order food."

Trouble hated one of his best friends right then. Lucky needed to work on his timing. "Fine, I'll get the pizza. But I want a date. An actual date without my friends around. Mina is welcome, but the assholes, they stay home next time."

"What about dinner at my place? I'm not a great cook, but you won't get food poisoning."

"You're probably a gourmet chef compared to me. I burned a pot and smoked up the house, I was banned from the kitchen."

"Okay, dinner, my place, Saturday?"

"I'll switch Saturdays, go inside, and I'll order pizza. Don't make eye contact with Lucky."

Brody slipped from between him and window, Trouble almost grabbed him again, but let him go. He pulled out his phone as he watched Brody disappear inside. Food and then he could get back inside to Brody and Mina. He took in the scene on the other side of the glass. Brody and Mina mixed with his friends and family. What he saw was everything he'd ever wanted and would never admit to even to the people he'd considered the most important people in his lives. He just had to convince Brody that he was more than a pretty face. He didn't know if he was up to the task. Trouble fucked up everything except in his safe place of Twirled World. He needed to be more than Jimmy

Carver the stupid fuck up—to have Brody see him as more than that.

He pushed a sigh passed his compressed lips and brought himself back to ordering dinner. He turned away from the sight in front of him and let the forced smile slip. For a minute, he wasn't going to pretend because he was getting damn tired of the facade. Wouldn't his friends get a laugh at the truth? Over confident and pretty Trouble frozen in fear of never being good enough to be loved.

# 4 WHAT THE HELL DID HE GET HIMSELF INTO?

Brody obsessively searched every inch of his apartment for specks of dust. Nervous energy had him cleaning all day, and nothing was out of place. Mina even had even put away all her toys in her room when she found out Trouble was coming for dinner. She'd asked were the guys coming with him. He'd had to tell her no. Thankfully, her disappointment hadn't lasted too long. At her age, she had the attention span of a gnat.

He'd thrown together a chicken and rice casserole that was easy, and Mina never complained about eating. As nervous as he was, he wanted the night to go well. Okay, it wouldn't be a normal date with his daughter in tow. Trouble shocked him when he said he didn't mind having Mina along, even though his wariness grew about her getting used to Trouble being around. Okay, he wasn't going to think about the breakup. A date didn't equal a lifelong commitment.

His last committed relationship hadn't gone as expected. Carla was his girlfriend all through high school when she'd gotten pregnant their senior year it seemed the logical step to get married after graduation. A year into the marriage so much changed. He worked days at the grocery store, and she took a waitressing job at night, so one of them always kept an eye on Mina.

Carla found friends through work and Mina became his best friend. She started staying out later. He began to suspect her of cheating, but he hadn't anticipated the drugs even though she used most weekends. Barely a year later, her parents stuck her in her first rehab facility. She refused to see him or Mina, she hadn't been ready for marriage or the kid, while he'd always thought one day he'd have kids.

When he and Carla had spoken, they were friendly, he'd wanted to try to stay friends, but in the end, they were affable when they talked. He couldn't say the same for his ex-in-laws. They weren't interested in Mina. It was going on a year since they'd even seen her. They'd moved to the West Coast three years ago. He and Eli tried to give her as normal a life as possible.

"I've never seen your place this clean," Elijah's voice startled him, and he turned to find his brother standing in the doorway of the living room.

"What are you doing here?"

"Wow, I'm feeling the love."

"Sorry, Trouble's coming over for dinner, and I'm trying to get the place—"

"You're having a date with Mina here?"

"Yes, why," Brody asked.

He straightened the pillows again and then forced himself away from the couch. Brody wanted their first date to go well. Even if it having Mina around didn't move

34

toward a traditional date. Trouble's acceptance of Mina's importance to him made him feel better about giving in to spending time with the other man.

"Normally dates are one on one affairs."

"How would you know? The last date I set you up on you chickened out before you walked through the restaurant door."

"I think he was old enough to be our father."

"He was not. He just had gray hair. You're too damn picky. It's why you're going to die single, and all your cats will consume your body before the neighbors question the smell."

"I don't have any cats."

Elijah pouting was a sight to see. His proper, upstanding member of society brother could turn into a tantrum throwing, overgrown toddler in nothing flat.

"Not yet."

"Do you want me to watch her tonight?"

"You'd do that?"

"Of course, this is the first person you've shown interest in since the divorce. He and his friends are weird, but they seem harmless, except for that Lucky person."

"He's interested in Priest, so I think you're safe."

Elijah shuddered, and Brody tried not to laugh. He loved his brother. The man raised him from the minute their parents brought Brody home from the hospital. Like Carla, he'd come from a well-to-do family with old money. Their mom and dad hadn't given up their partying lifestyle and left them in the care of nannies who only worked for a paycheck. None of the women who watched them spent any more time with them than necessary. In some ways, he believed their upbringing warped Elijah. He refused to open himself to the possibility of being loved and always found something wrong with the men he dated.

"Thank god, I was thinking of getting a chastity belt if I had to be in his presence again."

"He wasn't that bad." Okay, Lucky had the abrasive personality of sandpaper, but Lucky seemed harmless if a little eccentric.

"He wanted to take me in the back room." Elijah's voice rose several octaves.

He suspected Elijah's inexperience. He was more than a little repressed in the sex department. The sex speech Elijah gave him when Brody turned thirteen had turned his brother bright red, and Brody swore Elijah came close to a panic attack.

"I don't think he was serious." Brody moved toward his recliner and picked up the throw pillow, he started fluffing it.

"I'd prefer not to test your theory. Get Mina ready." As soon as Elijah spoke the doorbell rang.

"He's here." Brody froze with the pillow in his hands, and he proceeded to attempt to squeeze the stuffing out of it.

Elijah jerked the pillow from his hands and threw it back into the chair. Brody looked into his brother's eyes as Elijah shook him once, "Calm down, I'll get the door, and you'll pack Mina an overnight bag."

"I don't know, maybe I should—"

"It's been too damn long since you've gotten laid."

"I wasn't planning on getting laid. It's just a first date." Sex with Trouble sounded like a dangerous idea. Trouble made it clear he was attracted to him, but he didn't know— he wasn't going there. It wasn't the time to think about anything other than getting to know Trouble. "Have you seen him?"

"Yeah, yeah, he's too hot, and he's interested, so, quit arguing. We don't have time for this." Elijah spun him and pushed him toward the hallway.

"Go answer the damn door before he leaves," Brody took off to Mina's room. His apartment was small, so it was easy enough to listen to make sure Elijah didn't completely embarrass him.

"Hey, sweetie, Trouble's here, but Uncle Elijah wanted to know if you wanted to spend the night with him."

As soon as he said it her little bottom lip poked out and started to quiver. His daughter knew where to hit him to cause the most emotional pain.

"But, Daddy, I wanted to see Trouble."

"Okay, let's go see Trouble then." As much as he hated to admit it, he was relieved she wanted to stay. How sad was he that he needed a mini-chaperon?

She took off around him, and he spun to follow on her heels quickly.

"Trouble," she squealed and, as per Mina in her usual hyperactivity, launched herself at Trouble.

Trouble bent his knees and caught her, then twirled her around causing her to giggle.

"Princess, the guys and I got you something." Trouble knelt and pulled a paper bag from his battered backpack slung over one shoulder.

"Really?"

"Yeah," Trouble handed it to her.

Brody watched Trouble observe her with an expectant look on his face. Trouble almost seemed to be holding his breath. Brody turned his attention to Mina as she pulled out several flat packages.

"Temporary tattoos, something to hold you over until you can come back to the shop."

"Thank you!" Mina threw her arms around Trouble's neck and attempted to squeeze the life out of the man.

"Maybe after dinner, we can pick some."

"Daddy, look." She held them up with the biggest smile on her face.

"I see. Hi, Trouble."

"Hey, Brody." Trouble's deep voice caused his heartbeat to pick up. The other man stood and approached him. "I'm a little early, but I had to get out of the house. Lucky was being annoying."

"I can understand that."

Trouble hugged him and kissed his cheek. "Elijah said he was taking Princess for the night?" Trouble stepped back and gave him a look.

"Oh, she decided she didn't want to go. She's been looking forward to you having dinner with us."

"I was looking forward to spending time with y'all." Trouble stepped back.

Brody thought the man appeared nervous. With his confidence, it surprised him that Trouble would feel insecure.

"Don't you want to spend the night with me," Elijah asked.

"No, I want to have dinner with Trouble, and he's going to read me a story."

"Is he, did you ask if Trouble wanted to read you a bedtime story?"

"No." Mina's lip started again.

"Of course, I'll read her a bedtime story. We have tattoos to pick." Trouble lifted Mina up and perched her on his arm as they looked between Elijah and him.

He swore Trouble pouted his lip out as far as Mina's. Chuckling at Elijah's despondent expression for being turned down for a sleepover. His brother wasn't used to sharing his favorite person spot with other people, now he had to do it with six other people.

"Fine, then I'll leave you to your exciting night."

"Quit acting like your best friend decided she doesn't like you anymore."

"She doesn't. Look," Elijah pointed.

Trouble and Mina had their heads together. "You want a juice box," Mina asked.

"I'd love one."

Elijah snorted, and Brody chuckled as Trouble and Mina disappeared toward the kitchen.

"I'm going home."

"Don't be a baby," he yelled at his brother as the man headed for the door.

"Bye, Mina."

"The name's Princess," Mina answered, and Elijah slammed the door behind him.

What the hell has he gotten himself into? He went to join them in the kitchen.

✦ ✦ ✦

Mina threw him out of her bedroom so Trouble could read to her. It was odd to relax on the couch and have someone else taking care of the bedtime ritual of cuddles and story. All three of them laughed over dinner. He'd listened to stories about Trouble's friends and bosses. Trouble had focused intently on Mina whenever she spoke. He'd never experienced a night with someone that were typically family events.

Carla and him never actually shared dinner or worked as a team to get Mina into bed. Trouble had even seemed engrossed in Mina's favorite movie. If he wasn't careful, he could fall quickly for the incredibly sweet man.

"Is getting five books read to her the norm?"

He tipped his head back to look up at Trouble who stood behind the couch. Trouble's usually messy hair was even more mussed than normal. "If someone doesn't tell her no, then yes."

"How can you tell her no? I tried after book two, and that lip poked out. I mean, man, how can you tell that much cuteness no?"

"After five years, you get kind of used to it."

He watched Trouble walk around the opposite end of the couch and flop back, then he leaned to the side to rest his head on Brody's shoulder. He rested his cheek on the top of Trouble's soft hair. Long, strong fingers twined with his, and he froze as he waited—for what he didn't know.

"I couldn't get used to it."

"It would just take some practice."

"Can I ask you a question? I didn't want to ask in front of Princess."

He knew what was coming, but he agreed anyway. The questions about his ex would've come at some point, and he'd rather get them out the sooner, the better. "Sure, ask anything."

"Where's Mina's mom?"

"Rehab or at least that's the latest gossip. I don't keep in touch with the people Carla and I were friends with."

"Were you married?"

"Yeah, a few days before our two-year wedding anniversary the divorce became final."

"We're you together long?" Trouble's fingers squeezed between his and lifted his hand to Trouble's mouth.

"Aren't you just full of questions?"

Shit, he didn't mean for it to come out bitchy, but Brody didn't get asked about Carla. He figured that went with the whole dating situation.

"You don't have to answer."

"Sorry, I'm not used to all the questions." He rested his head back. "It's okay. We started dating our freshman year of high school, there was a broken condom our senior year."

"So, you did the responsible thing and got married?"

"We were planning for college and then she was late. Elijah begged me to go to college. He was going to pay for it, but I asked Carla to marry me instead. I don't think either of us was ready to be parents, but when Mina was born, I couldn't imagine not being a dad." Trouble's thumb stroked along his and then lifted Brody's hands to his lips again. "Carla got a job and with the job, new friends. She liked the drugs and alcohol in high school, but it got out of hand. Her parents found out and got her to go into treatment."

"You filed for divorce?"

"Actually she did and gave me full custody. It's not easy being a single parent. Some days the stress gets to be too much, and there's never enough money, but we get through."

"She's a great kid."

"Thanks, I didn't do too bad a job."

"No, you didn't."

Trouble's free hand came up and cupped his cheek, and turned his head. He licked his lips as his gaze fell to Trouble's masculine mouth.

"Say no," Trouble whispered.

Seconds after he shook his head firm lips pressed to his and his lids fell closed. He turned his upper body just as Trouble wrapped him in strong arms and traced his tongue along the seam of his lips. He groaned at the overwhelming pleasure of kissing Trouble. Too much time passed since he'd touched and had someone touch him. Trouble pushed him to his back and Trouble's heavyweight came to rest on his without ever breaking the contact.

"I can't have sex with you," he mumbled into Trouble's mouth.

"Of course not, it's our first date." Trouble's teeth nipped at his lower lip. "But I make no guarantees on the second one."

He nodded and laughed before it ceased when Trouble deepened the kiss. Right then, he didn't care if it was the first date or not, he'd give in to whatever Trouble wanted as long as the kiss didn't end. He wanted the man with an intensity he'd never experienced before, and he wasn't ready to give it up. Brody would push him away just not yet.

# 5 UNHAPPY FAMILY REUNION

Trouble pulled to the side of the road right before the turn to his parent's house. He'd fought the urge to puke since he woke that morning. It wasn't often they summoned him to the mansion for a family dinner. Most of the time they ignored his existence. He turned his upper body and opened the garment bag he'd stashed in his truck the night before. The suit cost more than he paid in rent and bills for six months and he instantly hated it.

It was bullshit and a lie, the suit wasn't him, but he had to force himself into it. He kicked off his untied boots and leaned down to throw them onto the passenger side floorboard. Quickly he stripped out of his clothes and replaced them with the day's costume. He ignored the jacket as he expertly knotted the conservative red tie with the tiny silver thread accents. Groaning as he felt it start to choke him. He pulled down the visor and combed his hair.

All he had to do was make it through the meal, and he'd go back to his real life. The piercings, the tunnels through his lobes and the visible tattoos couldn't be helped, he was as decent as he was getting. He restarted his truck and pulled forward to take the turn onto the long drive. When the house came into view, and he saw the vehicles lined up, great, it was a fucking party.

His siblings, their perfect spouses and kids were there, and it seemed several other people were too. "Trouble, you can do this, you can do this, you can—" Who the fuck was he kidding? The visit was going to be a slaughter. He just wondered how quickly they'd sacrifice him as a joke. He parked and reached for his phone, and he turned it to silent. One call and he knew the guys would storm the castle. Just the thought made him feel better even though he'd never said where he was going.

Brody had a short day on Saturdays maybe he could meet up with him and Mina. He was putting this shit off. *Get it over with!* If he were lucky, his mother would already be relaxed by a few Vodkas and Valiums. Exiting his truck, he grabbed his jacket and slipped it on, he tugged at the cuffs of his shirt and buttoned the three buttons. The dress shoes felt foreign as if he were playing dress up. He slammed the door and strode slowly toward the porch, then ascended the steps. Pausing at the door, he shook his shaking hands and reached out with his right hand to ring the bell.

The fact he had to hit the fucking doorbell at his old home caused his chest to tighten. He stepped back to wait for the housekeeper to answer.

When the door opened, he smiled at Greta.

"James, don't you look handsome."

"Hi, Greta, you don't change." He resisted the compulsion to hug the woman who practically raised him along with the disinterested nannies. "I received an invite."

A beautiful off-white card with his mother's perfect writing with a date and time.

"Mrs. Carver informed us you'd be attending today. Come on in, keep your jacket on everyone else is wearing one."

"I figured." He stepped in as she stepped back. It was like walking into a picture of one of those beautiful house magazines. He longed for the psychedelic walls of Twirled House with the mismatched furniture Lucky had reupholstered with Saris he'd bought in bulk. It wasn't perfect, but it was his home since almost the day Gib hired him.

"Everyone's out back in the garden."

"Thank you," he whispered as he forced his feet to move. He heard his steps echoing off the walls of the perfectly decorated mausoleum filled with expensive reminders of the generations before that were just a little less rich.

Trouble stepped out onto the back patio. He looked over the gardens with their colorful flowers, the hedge maze he'd hidden inside as a child and statues of naked cherubs. Fake Jesus, it was painful, and he wanted nothing to do with it.

"James, glad to see you arrived," His father's disappointed tone felt like a punch to the gut. Either he was a minute late, or James Senior was hoping he wouldn't come at all.

"Hello, Dad, I received Mother's invitation."

"Couldn't you have done something to cover those horrid marks?"

He inwardly flinched and automatically reached up to touch the ink on his neck, catching sight of the ones on his hands. "Sorry."

"You're always sorry, James. Go see your mother. I'm sure she wants to check you over."

He simply nodded and went in search of his mother. Check him over would entail her insulting the suit he had barely been able to afford and finding it lacking. Along with his tattoos, hair, piercings, job and the fact he didn't bring a guest with tits.

Trouble spotted her quickly holding court, he looked around finding his brother and sister sitting nearby with their plastic spouses and children. His nieces and nephews wouldn't dare get a stain on their clothes. He'd wait to greet that family nightmare later.

"Excuse me, Mother."

Cold, dead blue eyes rose to his but not before they stroked from his high polished shoes to his perfectly groomed hair. No one else would've noticed but that calculating and disapproving stare stopped on each of his tattoos and piercings.

"James, we expected you a half an hour ago."

"Forgive me." He swallowed as nausea made his mouth fill with saliva.

Trouble knew damn well he wasn't fucking late, but no one dared contradict Marla Carver. His mother introduced him to the group around her, and he caught the hesitation before saying son, as if admitting he was hers was disgusting. With the introductions out of the way, he was dismissed and sent toward his siblings to say hi. He'd rather have his Ampallang ripped out. He cringed and almost grabbed his dick at the thought.

"Jennifer, Joshua." He nodded at his siblings.

"James, surprised you had the nerve to show up. I know Mother sent that invite out of pity." Jennifer sneered at him.

"And to come looking like that, don't you have any shame? You're ridiculous."

Trouble tried not to bite through his tongue to keep from saying anything. If he did, they'd just make it worse. He'd be accused of making a scene and publicly shamed in front of the all the guests.

They'd hated him growing up, almost as much as his parents. It was made quite clear at every opportunity he was the reason their parents had to get married. James Senior couldn't keep it in his pants and cheated on his college girlfriend. He'd gotten Marla pregnant and to save from a scandal, James Senior had to marry her. His Dad kept his very miserable wife happy with plenty of presents and an unlimited shopping budget while he fucked every beautiful little secretary and intern he could bend over his desk.

"As always it was nice seeing you two again." He turned slowly and headed toward the maze, slipping through the entrance, he reached for his phone.

There was a text from Brody. He violently wiped at his eyes as he realized tears were streaking down his cheeks. Unlocking his phone, he clicked on the message icon and opened it. A video started.

"Trouble, look," Mina squealed and turned her cheek toward the camera. She had a little dragon tattoo on her cheekbone. "Daddy says I can't have one when I grow up, but I told him Trouble'd let me."

The phone tilted and Brody's cute face came into view with a glare aimed his way and shook his head. The camera jerked back to Mina's beautiful face.

"Daddy's making mac and cheese for dinner, ya gotta come." Mina plopped onto Brody's lap.

"You've gotta, she's driving me crazy with Trouble this, Trouble that. You're probably working but call or text me later." They both waved and the video ended.

Without thought he called Brody, it rang a few times, and then Brody answered. "She's not getting a face tattoo, Trouble." He could hear the laughter in the other man's voice.

Trouble tried to answer, but his voice broke.

"Trouble, what's wrong?"

"They hate me."

"Who hates you?"

"My family, I was sent an invite to dinner and they—"

"Get in your truck and come here."

"I can't, they'll—"

"I don't care what they'll do, come on, we'll watch some cartoons, eat boxed mac and cheese, and you'll tell Mina she can never have a face tattoo."

"Brody—"

"Trouble, we want you here, okay?"

"Okay, I'll be there soon."

"We'll be waiting."

Trouble disconnected the call and took the long way around the house. One minute he was getting into his truck and the next he was parking in front of Brody's apartment. He found himself running toward Brody's door, he barely reached the door, and it was already open. Brody stood there and opened his arms, Trouble stepped into them and lifted the smaller man off his feet.

"That suit is so wrong. Where's your real clothes?"

He tightened his embrace. "In the truck."

"Go inside with Mina, and I'll get your clothes, then you can change."

He set Brody back on his feet. Soft hands framed his face and even softer lips pressed to his. It didn't make the pain go away, but it eased it some. Brody dragged him inside and then left him.

"Did you go to church?" Mina stood in front of him her fists on her hips.

"No, can I have a hug, I've had a bad day."

In Mina fashion, she launched herself at him, and he caught her. "You don't look like you. I don't like it."

"I don't either, Princess. What ya watching?"

"Dragons, come on." She grabbed his hand as he set her down and he followed behind her.

He sensed Brody when the other man walked into the room.

"Trouble's going to change clothes." He turned to find Brody holding out a pile of clothes with his battered boots on top. "We have a burning barrel out back. You want to burn that monstrosity you're wearing?"

"I'd love too, but I gotta see if I can return it first."

"Okay, but if not, we can burn it."

Trouble stepped forward and took the clothes leaning down to kiss Brody. "Thanks."

"Don't mention it."

He passed Brody and headed for the bathroom to change into his real clothes, to be Trouble again and not stupid, disappointing James Carver Jr. He felt his eyes start burning again and he choked back the beginning of a sob. Was it too fucking much to ask to be enough just one time?

# 6 BRODY'S EPIPHANY

Brody curled up in his recliner and watched Trouble sleep on the couch with Mina laying on his chest. The sound of Trouble's voice broken by tears tore him apart. He'd never seen Trouble with anything but a smile on his face but the sadness in his ice blue eyes when he'd shown up at Brody's house earlier was something he'd never forget. Trouble hadn't spoken about what happened while he was at his parents.

How could parents treat their child to the point of making them feel hated? He should get up and take Mina to bed. It was odd how much he liked seeing Trouble with Mina. They'd quickly bonded, and that alone should fill him with trepidation. One of the main reasons he hadn't put in more effort to date was he didn't want Mina to become attached.

He just couldn't bring himself to keep them apart. Hell, he couldn't keep her away from the rest of the

Twirled Crew. It had only been Elijah, Mina and him for so long he'd never pictured other people in their lives.

His phone rang softly, and he answered it knowing it was Elijah. "Don't you have anything better to do," he whispered.

"No, I'm bored, but I wouldn't be if you two would come live with me. And why are you whispering?"

"Trouble and Mina are asleep on the couch."

"He's there again, doesn't he have his own place?"

"Quit being bitchy."

"I'm not bitchy.

"Yeah."

"I'm generally invited over for mac and cheese Saturdays, Mina didn't call me."

"You really have to stop acting like someone stole Mina from you."

"They have, I'm no longer the fun uncle, she has all those tattooed, motorcycle riding uncles now. All I hear about is Trouble this and Trouble that, or a repeat with Lucky, Scary, Priest, Zerk, even Landon. I've lost rank."

"From what I hear, Lucky's invited you out to their house a few times."

Elijah gasped, "I'm not going anywhere near him. He came to City Hall and tried to get into my office, my secretary almost had a heart attack when he told her he was there to see the sexy Mayor and asked was there a sturdy lock on the door. I never thought I'd get him to leave."

"He's a little odd, but he's harmless, I think."

"There's nothing harmless about that man. I believe he's taken way too many knocks to the head. He isn't right."

"But I think he has a thing for Priest so you should be safe."

Brody shifted in his chair and switched his phone to his other ear. He pushed a heavy sigh passed his lips. He didn't have the energy to deal with Elijah.

"I feel sorry for Priest. He seems like the sweetest one of that group."

"Did you just call to bitch about no longer being Mina's favorite, Lucky's fascination with trying to sleep with you or is there a reason you're bothering me at ten o'clock at night?"

"Mina starts her first day of school in a few weeks, I was wondering if I could be there when you drop her off?"

"Of course you can. It's her first day of school."

"Good and, Brody, please tell me you're being safe. We've had the talk."

He groaned and scrubbed his free hand over his face; Brody didn't want to have a repeat of the awkward sex talk.

"I'm not thirteen, Elijah, I know where the condom aisle is. I do work at a grocery store."

"Smart ass, you know what I mean."

"I'm nowhere near breaking my abstinence streak, so your delicate sensibilities are safe."

"Thanks, I'd rather not walk in on anything. I've heard those heathens talk."

"What are you, eighty? Because last time I checked, thirty-two was a little too young for grumpy old man status. You need to find yourself a boyfriend."

"I don't need some man cluttering up my life. I've got enough problems without one."

"You don't know what you're missing. Sex would loosen you up."

"I do fine on my own."

Anything having to do with sex made Elijah uncomfortable. It made him feel guilty his brother raised him and put his entire life on hold. Brody couldn't come close to showing his brother his appreciation.

"Ross Palm and his five brothers aren't exactly a fulfilling sex life." His eyes flew to the couch when he heard a snort and found Trouble grinning.

"Can we stop talking about this?"

"You brought it up."

"My mistake. Now I'm going to bed."

"Are your batteries fully charged?"

Trouble's soft, deep laughter drew his attention back to the couch. The man's blue eyes shined in the dimness of the living room.

"I'm almost embarrassed that I raised you."

"Come on, you don't mean that," Brody whined.

"I do, now, good night, and don't do anything I wouldn't do."

"Um, you do nothing, and that doesn't exactly sound like fun. I'm going to put Mina to bed and head that way myself, I have an early shift tomorrow."

"Need me to come pick Mina up?"

Trouble waved from the couch and pointed at his chest, mouthing the word, please. Oh man, Trouble's blue eyes pleaded with him.

"No, that's okay, Trouble said he'd watch her." He resisted the urge to chuckle at Trouble's little fist pump and then grimace when Mina mumbled in her sleep.

"Oh, well then. I'll call you later on in the week."

"Night, Elijah, and stop pouting."

"I'm not pouting." Elijah ended the call.

He chuckled. His brother didn't know how to share. Elijah was an only child until he was twelve.

"Your brother has some major sexual frustration going on."

"You have no idea." He dropped his feet to the floor and stood, walking over to the couch. "Let me put her to bed." He bent over, slipped his arms under Mina until he could lift her and cradle her against his chest.

He carefully walked toward Mina's room. If she woke up, it would be like she took a power nap and never go back to sleep. Her nightlight dimly illuminated her room, and he eased her onto the bed. Thankfully he forgot to make it that morning. His daughter always had her days and nights mixed up. It turned into a constant struggle when she was an infant to keep her on a regular schedule. That hadn't changed in the last five years.

He watched as she snuggled under her covers. Her dark hair was a mess against her pillows. Brody never saw much of his ex in Mina. Carla was blonde with dark chocolate colored eyes.

"She's beautiful, Brody."

Brody glanced over his shoulder to find a shirtless Trouble standing in the doorway. Dark blond hair covered his chest and thinned to a line between deep cut abs. Wow, Trouble was gorgeous, what the hell was he doing in his apartment? Unbuttoned jeans hung low on lean hips, exposing a V of muscle that showed a thick yet trimmed nest of pubic hair.

"You're staring." Trouble observed him with an odd expression. He almost appeared as if he were self-conscious.

"You have to know you're perfect."

"I know I'm pretty and not that smart."

"I'm not your family." He said it to ease Trouble's mind, but instead, he barely caught the subtle flinch as if Brody struck him.

"I know."

He walked away from Mina's bed and approached Trouble. He slipped his arms around Trouble and rested his cheek against the surprisingly soft chest hair. "Whatever you're thinking, that's not what I meant."

"Sorry, it's been a shit day, well, not all of it. I got to spend most of it with you and Princess."

"It was nice having you around." He lifted onto his toes and pressed his lips to Trouble's. A groan rumbled against his mouth as the man's strong arms tightened around him then walked them backward into the hall. Trouble pressed him back to the wall beside the door. Trouble's mouth slanted across his and his tongue insistently nudged at the seam. He parted letting Trouble inside. Damn, that was what he's missed the most about having someone, just being able to touch and kiss. Trouble gripped his waist and lifted. Brody momentarily stiffened until he relaxed and twined his legs around Trouble's hips locking his ankles.

"Don't you dare drop me," he ordered without taking breaking contact with Trouble's soft lips.

"Not a fucking chance. Have I mentioned how beautiful you are?"

"Men shouldn't be beautiful."

"Who says?" Trouble's fingertips traced his jaw and then his thumbs stroked over his lower lip. "You're perfect. First time I saw you I thought so. You kept saying no."

"You're gorgeous, and I'm just me."

"I haven't look at another man since."

He almost called him a liar until he peered into Trouble's eyes and saw the truth there. Brody couldn't speak. He felt Trouble start to shift, then lower him. He squeezed his legs around Trouble and raised his hands to place them on Trouble's scruffy cheeks. Trouble's eyes closed and he traced the man's long lashes with his thumbs. Again, he was amazed by Trouble wanting him. Trouble could have anyone, and he wanted plain, old Brody, a single father who barely made it to each paycheck.

He leaned forward, kissed each closed eye, across his high cheekbones and then to the corners of his sensual mouth.

"I can't believe you want me," he whispered.

"A lot, I want you." Trouble's hips jerked, and the thick ridge of his hard cock rubbed against his. "A lot."

"I can't, not yet." He regretted the need to say no, but it was years since he had a relationship and that one hadn't gone so great.

Trouble's forehead came to rest against his. "I better head to bed…well the couch."

Brody loosened his legs and let Trouble set him down. He couldn't mistake Trouble's disappointment or his own. Saying no took all the control he had.

"Do you want some more covers?"

Trouble backed away to press his back against the opposite wall. The space between them felt like miles.

"Naw, I'm good with the one. I can go home if it makes you more comfortable."

"You're fine right where you are. Do you really want to watch Mina tomorrow?"

"Yeah, I can take her to Twirled House. I'll have to sit out the morning ride, but that's no biggie. If it's okay with you maybe, I'll follow along in the truck, and she can have lunch with all of us."

"I don't see that as a problem."

"Thanks, you better get to bed and me too, I don't do well with mornings. Kinda not a requirement with my job."

"I can call—"

"No, it'll be great, and she'll have fun. You can pick her up at the house when you're done with work, or you can stay for dinner, we normally have that at Scary's place."

"I don't know, would he mind?"

"Naw, he likes Princess. She'll get to meet Tank."

"Who's Tank?"

"Oh, Scary's business partner and head of security at Brawlers. Nice enough guy, doesn't talk, but all of us know sign language. Maybe Princess would like to learn. I can find her some movies and flash cards, maybe Lucky still has the ones we used."

"I think she'd like that."

"Okay, well, good night." Trouble stepped forward and gave him a quick kiss before turning to walk away.

"Trouble," he called out.

Trouble turned back to him, "Yeah?"

"Sleep with me."

"What?"

"The couch isn't comfortable, I may not be ready for the sex, but I'd like—"

"Okay."

"I'm just going to get ready for bed. My room's at the end of the hall. I'll be there in a minute."

Trouble nodded and passed Brody heading for Brody's room. He didn't know what came over him, but he wanted Trouble in his bed even if they didn't take the step both of them obviously wanted. Quickly he made it through his usual routine, but cut his shower time in half. The longer he took, the more nervous he became. He changed into his pajama bottoms and t-shirt he'd hung from the towel rack earlier.

He turned off the bathroom light, then went to make sure everything was turned off and locked up. Padding barefoot through his apartment toward his bedroom and hesitated outside the bedroom door.

"Brody," Trouble called his name which got him moving.

"Sorry, I wanted to make sure everything was off."

"You can change—"

"I'm not changing my mind." He had stepped into the room before he did just that. Trouble smiled as he held the covers up. Brody crossed to the bed and slipped onto the bed next to Trouble. He turned his back to Trouble and scooted back into the cradle of the other man's muscular frame.

Trouble wrapped his arm around him and tugged him tighter to his frame.

"Good night," Trouble whispered and kissed the side of his neck.

"Night." He closed his eyes and felt himself relax. Smiling he inhaled the scent of incense that seemed to cling to the entire crew, but it smelled different on Trouble—sexier. Sleep would be a long time coming. Tomorrow was going to suck, yet he wouldn't regret a night in Trouble's arms.

# 7 WAS THIS HOW IT FELT TO HAVE A FAMILY?

"Kill it." He sleepily groaned as he tried to kill his alarm. He was going to kill Lucky for setting it for six a.m., the bastard was cruel. He'd tack Lucky's hairy ass to the wall like a fucking trophy.

"Don't kill my alarm," Brody's sleepy voice instantly brought him awake as a rough cheek stroked over his bare chest then Brody buried his head under Trouble's arm. The cute man's breath teased his ribs. He turned to wrap his arms tighter around Brody and nuzzled the top of his head.

"Who gets up this early? There's gotta be laws."

"Not all of us have jobs we don't have to be at until noon."

"Sometimes I gotta be there at eleven."

"Lucky you, but I have to get up."

"No, call in sick," he whined as he hooked his hand behind Brody's thigh and pulled it over his hip.

Brody laughed and lifted his head. "I can't afford to miss a day, groceries, bills and gas don't buy themselves."

"Adulting sucks." He pushed Brody's shaggy hair back from his flushed face and sleepy eyes.

"People have to adult."

"Still doesn't mean it's right." He was about to lower his mouth to Brody's when tiny feet approached quickly down the hallway. Brody tried to put distance between their bodies, and he wasn't going to let that happen. The door flew open and, in Mina-style, jumped onto the bed.

"Trouble, you and Daddy had a sleepover."

Mina laid down on top of them and wiggled until she was between them.

"Morning, Princess." He couldn't help smiling as she used both hands to push her heavy mop of hair away from her face. She cuddled down beside him as he caught Brody shaking his head.

"Mina, what are you doing up so early?"

Brody kissed the top of Mina's head before he rolled out of bed.

"I'm not sleepy." Mina took over Brody's half of the bed and settled her little head on his pillow.

"You're never sleepy."

"Am I going to Uncle Eli's house?"

"Nope, you're spending the day with me."

"Will I get to see the guys?"

"Yep."

She squealed and launched herself at him. Brody strode from the bedroom toward the bathroom mumbling to himself.

"But the guys are still asleep, so we need to lay down for just a little bit longer."

"But, Trouble, I'm—"

"Just close your eyes, and I promise I'll wake you up to get ready."

"Promise."

"You know I will."

She grabbed the covers and pulled them up to her pointed chin and rolled over until she curled against his chest. Her curls tickled his stubbly chin. Trouble laid there listening to the shower running down the hall and Mina's breaths slowly evening out. He'd rarely slept over especially after a night of only sleeping.

He eased away from Mina and made sure she stayed asleep. Trouble threw his legs over the side of the mattress, then leaned over and picked his jeans from the foot of the bed. He stepped into the worn fabric and slid them on, he zipped them but left them unbuttoned. Tip-toeing from the bedroom and stepped into the hall, then walked toward the bathroom to lean back against the wall beside the door. It opened, and steam billowed out, Brody appeared with a towel knotted around his waist and hung low on his hips. Water beaded on his pale skin and for the first time, he got a look at Brody's perfect smooth skin. Brody's soft stomach subtly curved.

"I'm done if you—"

"I put Mina back to sleep. Now, what were we doing...oh yeah." Trouble reached out and grabbed Brody's hips to tug him close. He leaned heavier against the wall to pull Brody into the cradle of his thighs.

"I don't—"

He settled his mouth over Brody's to cut off his protest. The smaller man moaned as their lips and skin connected. Brody still slightly damp from his shower shivered in his arms. Parting his lips, he pushed at the seam of Brody's mouth as Brody instantly opened for him slanting his head a little, allowing Trouble to deepen the kiss.

Brody's dick hardened against his, and he stroked his right hand up Brody's back to curve his hand around his nape. Holding and kissing Brody was unlike anything he'd ever experienced before, and he was quickly coming to crave everything about Brody.

Ending the kiss with gentle nips, then resting his forehead to Brody's he took a breath inhaling the clean scent of soap, shampoo and toothpaste. His scent was like home.

"You're not playing fair, Trouble, I have to go to work." Brody stepped back to put space between them.

He couldn't resist grinning at Brody's retreat.

"I know, but I wanted a kiss before you left."

"You're weird."

"Um, you have met my friends."

"True."

"I'm going to take a shower while Mina's sleeping and then give Scary a call."

"Okay." Brody lifted onto his toes and pressed his lips to Trouble's quickly before quickly heading back to his bedroom. "Towels are in the cabinet beside the sink."

He turned and stepped into the bathroom closing the door behind him. Stripping his jeans and boxer briefs, he reached around the curtain to turn the water on. He wondered if that was what it was like to be part of a couple—a family? His insecurities chose that moment to come viciously roaring back and made him wonder when he'd fuck it up like he always did. Would Brody come to hate him as much as his family? He hoped not because it was too soon, yet he could see himself falling hard for Brody and raising Mina.

He waved off the offer of a second beer from Lucky. One more wouldn't fuck with him, but it didn't feel right drinking in front of Princess. Right then, she was sitting on Scary's bike with the big man behind her as he revved the engine making her giggle. No one would've thought the big, menacing man would be good with a kid, much less a girl, but as soon as Scary knew Princess was coming, he'd taken over.

Tank set on the porch steps close by. He'd known the silent man as long as he had Scary, but they didn't interact much. He'd noticed Princess sending side-eyed glances in Tank's direction. For grown ass men, it was terrifying to approach Tank, so for a small slip of a girl—Princess patted Scary's arm to signal she wanted down.

As soon as her tiny sneakers hit the ground, she was off in Tank's direction. He watched her carefully, he knew Tank wouldn't do anything to hurt her, but he didn't want her feelings hurt when Tank couldn't respond.

"Hi, my name is Mina, can you teach me to spell my name?"

"Princess," he called her name.

"Please."

Tank's face brightened, and a half-smile tilted his mouth.

"You're getting good at all this shit," Lucky staged whispered and earned a rough shout of his name from Scary.

"You're asking to get your ass kicked today, man."

"Just like any other day. Ruin all the sexy hippie's fun."

"You're not gonna get Priest all hot for your unwashed hippie ass if you don't start acting like a fucking adult."

"Priest loves me as is, he just hasn't figured it out yet."

"Lucky," Priest admonished as he passed on his way from his bike to the house.

"Sorry, dear."

"You're like an old married couple."

"I couldn't be so lucky."

He laughed at Lucky's miserable sigh. Maybe Lucky wasn't so clueless about the chemistry between Lucky and Priest. The crew always joked about the two men, but it had always been in fun. They were opposites; the thought of Priest and Lucky together was terrifying.

His phone beeped to signal a new text. He stroked his fingertips across the screen to unlock it.

Brody: *Replacement running late. Be another hour. OK?*

Trouble: *K. Tank's teaching her to cuss in ASL.*

He hit send and listened to Lucky laugh beside him.

"He's gonna leave work early whether his backup shows or not. People say I'm fucking Trouble. Ew, that didn't sound right."

"No, and please for the love of Fake Baby Jesus, never say it again."

"Deal. I think I threw up in my mouth a bit. I need another beer." Lucky lunged from his chair and rushed to the cooler on the porch.

Brody: *You're not funny.*

Trouble: *She's cool. Having fun. Grill goes hot in 90.*

Brody: *Okay.*

He put his phone away and slouched low in his chair laying his head back against the rough fabric.

"You're on grill duty, Trouble, no time for a—a nap."

He snorted at Scary censoring himself. He hoped never to see six a.m. ever again. How Brody did it and then chased around an active five-year-old was beyond him. The man was a fucking beast because Trouble was about to pass the fuck out. "Got any energy drinks," he asked as he lifted his head and caught Scary's eye.

"Inside."

Trouble groaned as he pushed to his feet and headed for the house, he had to pass Tank and Princess, so he leaned down and kissed Mina's soft hair. He straightened and headed inside, chug a few cans of high-octane caffeine and he'd be good to go—he hoped.

# 8 INTERACTING WITH THE NATIVES

Brody was nervous. He'd hung out with Trouble's friends and co-workers before, but he had the buffer of Elijah or Mina. Mina was already there although she tended to run off to spend time with the guys. They treated her like the Princess they nicknamed her even as she asked endless questions, studied their tattoos and piercings as if they were canvases gracing the walls of museums. He was sure she'd seen tattoos before, yet until she'd met the Twirled Crew, she'd never reached the levels of obsessed.

They'd quickly become her honorary Uncles, and it was nice to have people other than Elijah to share Mina. He'd tried play groups and other activities where she'd spend time with other kids and it hadn't ever worked. His daughter was open and friendly, well-adjusted, but she didn't relate to her peers. In pre-school, she hadn't mentioned one kid, in particular, she'd played with or called a friend.

He followed the directions Trouble texted him and turned left onto Hayes, he passed five houses until he got to the one with Trouble's truck and several motorcycles parked out front. It was a bungalow style that fit with the others on the block. He parked at the curb and observed the men sitting and walking around, they were all huge. It was like arriving in the land of Giants and Mina was right in the middle of it.

She was engrossed in some conversation with a mean looking man in the sleeveless t-shirt with what looked like an exploding skull on the front and holey jeans. For some reason, he found the large bare feet odd. A huge pair of black boots were lined neatly on the step beside him.

He was making movements with his hands like American Sign Language, and Mina would copy them a little less deftly. Then it dawned on him that must be the silent Tank.

"She's been attached to him for the last hour," Trouble's voice coming through his open window startled him.

"He's not really teaching her to cuss, is he?"

"No, just basics. Kind of like please, thank you, the signs for objects. He was working on the ABCs earlier, that sort of shit. We've been helping here and there, but she hasn't paid much attention to us."

"She's not treating him like a new toy?" He almost groaned.

"I think Tank's enjoying it, we've seen him smile a few times. Come on and keep me company while I man the grill. It's my weekend."

"I don't want to intrude. I can just get Mina and—"

"You're fine. Mina helped us grocery shop."

"You didn't get her everything she asked for, did you?"

Trouble turned away and rocked on his heels.

"She wanted to know about the just her size baby steaks."

"You mean Filet Mignon?"

"Maybe."

"Those sometimes cost more than my grocery budget for a day."

"Don't fuss at me, Lucky bought it for her."

"My sweet baby girl is gonna be spoiled."

"All she knows is it's a steak her size. No big deal. Once in a while won't hurt."

"Fine, I'm not arguing."

"Good, now come into the backyard. It's lonely back there."

"Why's everyone in the front yard?"

"Zerk and Scary were tuning up their bikes. Lucky was trying to kill himself on his board, then tried to teach Mina how to do some tricks. She'll want a skateboard soon."

"A motorcycle, face tattoo and now a skateboard, y'all are turning my child into a daredevil."

"Could be worse."

He watched Trouble shrug before Trouble opened his door. He removed his keys and slid from the seat pocketing the keyring as Trouble pulled him in for a kiss.

"Aw hell yeah, dinner and a dirty show," Lucky crooned from behind them.

He broke the kiss and looked over his shoulder to see Lucky with his arms resting on the roof and his chin on his stacked hands. He waggled his eyebrows causing the sun to catch in the pierced one.

"Hello, Lucky, I hear you're spoiling Mina."

"Naw, but we were looking at boards online until Priest confiscated the laptop."

"I'll thank him later."

"Whatever."

"Daddy," Mina squealed, and he caught sight of her running across the yard. She had on a mini Twirled World Ink t-shirt and tiny combat boots.

He wasn't going to argue, he mentally repeated. He was still unsure of how long the guys would be in her life. His biggest worry about meeting someone was her getting used to someone he was dating, now he had to worry about the addition of Uncles.

"You're thinking negative shit, so stop it," Trouble whispered and stepped away.

He opened his mouth to respond, but Mina cut him off when she threw her arms around his legs. Brody leaned over to pick her up and took in her wide, bright smile.

"Have you been good today?"

"Yep, we went to the grocery store, shopping and got me new shoes and a shirt, just like the guys."

He couldn't be mad with her so happy and excited. "Did you say thank you?"

"Yes," she stated proudly.

"Good girl."

"Tank's been teaching me talk with my hands. I've got movies and flash cards too."

"We gave her the disks and flash cards we learned from."

"Tank says she's a natural." Lucky came around the car and plucked Mina from his arms. "We're gonna go torture Priest. I'm trying to talk him into reproducing with me."

"We already said that's impossible," Trouble hollered after him while laughing.

"Maybe Lou will rent us some womb space."

"I so want to be around for that conversation."

Lucky flipped Trouble off over his shoulder as Lucky and Mina headed in Priest's direction.

"Lou?"

Trouble twined their fingers and dragged him toward the narrow path between the two-car garage and the house. It opened into a surprisingly large backyard. Two picnic tables set under the shade of a large tree not far from a monstrous smoking grill. He bit his lip as he noticed the dragon painted on the side letting smoke flow from the vents.

"Lucky's twin, she's a hard ass commitment-phobe. The thought of having babies gives her hives. He also has a brother named Linus."

"Linus?"

Trouble pulled a lawn chair over and settled him into it as Trouble positioned himself in front of the grill. It still felt weird not to be checking on Mina every few minutes, but he had to admit it was nice.

"Yep, they give him blankets for every birthday, last year I think it was a custom one with two men in a very compromising position. He's normal, and the whole family lives to torture him. Lucky's mom swears she adopted him from the Norm store."

"So, Lucky's—"

"Every one of them is insane. Damon, Lucky's dad, was pretty normal until Lily got her claws into him. He's a professor of Gender Studies."

"Did Mina sleep long after I left?"

"Maybe an hour. I took her to Twirled and let her loose on the crew to wake them up. She was asking why Priest was asleep with Lucky."

"Oh."

"He sometimes has nightmares, and Lucky lets him sleep in his bed. They had on clothes. She didn't have a problem with us, so we just told her the truth. Zerk and Landon's door was thankfully locked, but she can bang on a door like the cops getting ready to come in though." Trouble chuckled and opened the lid, flipping steaks.

"Thank you for today."

"No problem. It was great, and she had fun. Thanks for trusting me."

"You're welcome." There was an odd sadness in Trouble's gaze before the man quickly hid it and went back to his usual smiling self. He wondered how much damage Trouble's family caused over the years. There was no conceivable notion why they'd treat a sweet man like Trouble the way they did. Yes, he didn't look normal and didn't act it most of the time, but he was caring, gorgeous and perfect with Mina.

As the guys and Mina roamed from the front yard conversations switched to funny stories of working at Twirled and their antics. He learned they'd changed their Sunday routine to accommodate Mina and canceled their usual morning ride. He'd wanted to protest, yet they didn't seem to mind. Instead, they'd done things to include Mina.

He felt slightly guilty that he'd denied spending time with Trouble before and the only reason he had was that of a packed diner. Mina played musical laps going from one crew member to another, except for Zerk and Landon where she had to sit on Landon's lap while he sat on Zerk's. He was jealous of the obvious love between the two men. They touched and kissed all the time with no fear of reprisal. The Twirled Crew were all gay, so it was understandable, but the first time he'd met them, the two men were in the same position.

The other surprising thing was the interaction between Lucky and Priest, although it was more subtle. They assured him they were best friends, but the way they unconsciously sought each other out to touch or just be near the other proved something else. That's when he noticed it, Trouble sat beside him with his hand on Brody's thigh. He hadn't even noticed his hand rested on top of Trouble's as if it were the natural thing to do.

The rest of the night progressed the same. Conversation, food and a lot of laughs. He felt included as if he'd known them years instead of mere weeks. As the sun set, they moved downstairs to what turned out to be a home bar and rec room. The guys took turns teaching Mina to play pool while a Disney movie played.

He found himself getting closer to Trouble the entire night until he curled under the man's muscled, tattooed arm close to dozing off. He'd never felt that way with his ex. Yes, he loved her, and they were affectionate, but they never just sat around with friends, just comfortable and content. He wondered if this was what it was like to be secure and happy? If it was, he was coming to like it a bit too much as his fear of the unknown future plagued the dark recesses at the back of his mind. He mentally shook it off, he wouldn't worry about it yet, he'd just enjoy it and if nothing else happened maybe he'd finally found a group of friends all his own.

# 9 THE FIRST GROWN UP DATE

He was about to lose his shit. Trouble tugged at the front of his white button up dress shirt and checked himself in the mirror. He ran his fingers through his hair and wondered if it was time for a haircut, it was getting a bit long on top. Fuck, he hated worrying about that shit. Yeah, everyone thought he had his shit together, maybe that he was some player. He didn't want to think about the men from his past. Most of them were a sad way of trying to feel wanted—needed.

Even if no one wanted the whole package, at least for a little while, someone wanted a piece of him. No matter how he hated it the morning after, for a brief moment—he shook off the thoughts that were going to depress him. Tonight was his first official date with Brody. Because of Brody's schedule, they had to go this evening, Monday wasn't exactly a hot date night, but it's what they had.

They hadn't been able to see each other in a week. Texts and phone calls were as good as it got, and Trouble called at Princess's bedtime so he could tell her good night. He didn't know how great of an idea it was to get so attached to both of them. Wearing out his welcome was a skill he'd cultivated to perfection since his birth.

He checked the black leather cuff watch with the skull studs and saw he had thirty minutes to make it to Brody's. Elijah volunteered to babysit, but he'd heard there was a lot of pouting on Elijah's part about all the time he was missing with his niece. He and the guys may have taken over Uncle time, but the few times they'd invited Elijah over, he'd declined.

He glanced down to check to make sure his best leather boots weren't scuffed. On his way to the door, he grabbed his wallet and keys off the dresser.

"Looking sexy, pretty boy." Lucky whistled from the open door of his room. "You look almost fuck-able all spiffed up."

"Fuck you."

"Is that an offer?" Lucky leered and waggled his brows.

Priest passed shaking his head as he slipped into Lucky's room. "Lucky, leave him alone." Priest smiled at him. "Ignore him and go have fun with your man."

"Thanks, Priest."

He liked the man, he was the newbie of the crew by a few years. Priest kept some heavy secrets they were sure, and they were convinced the man had to be completely insane to spend almost every hour of the day with Lucky.

He put his crazy roommates out his mind as he jogged down the steps, then out the front door. He thought about taking the bike, but he hadn't gotten Brody to agree to a ride yet. His *Chevy* would have to do. He hopped into the driver's seat, felt a bit of calm at the rumble of the engine and took off to pick up Brody.

It was only about a twenty-minute drive across town to Brody's apartment, but with his nerves, it felt like it took three times that. It was their first grown-up date, and he wanted it to be perfect. They'd only shared a few kisses, one short make out session and one innocent night of sleeping together—which was new for him. Most of their time together had been spent with Mina or hanging out with his friends.

He pulled into the space beside Brody's car. The place he'd picked was a small Italian place within walking distance, Vince, the chef, was a regular at Twirled. He got out and locked the door, pocketed his keys and headed for the door. As always Brody opened the door and waited for him with a welcoming smile.

He wondered if it would always be like that, Brody always there to welcome him home, but the thought frightened him. The idea of getting his hopes too high and having Brody decide—not thinking about it.

"Mina wouldn't leave until she got to see you." Brody exasperated tone held a hint of amusement.

"Is Elijah's heartbroken," Trouble asked as he leaned down to press a kiss to Brody's smile. "You look fucking gorgeous."

Brody's face turned the cutest shade of pink. "He swears you and the crew knocked him out of favorite uncle position."

"We're cooler, what can I say?"

"There's the Trouble ego I've missed this last week."

"Missed you too," Trouble said as he walked through the door. "Princess," he called out and chuckled at the squeal that could've shattered glass.

"Trouble, do I have to go to Uncle Elijah's house? Can we stay with the crew? Lucky's fun."

He swung Princess into his arms and tried not to laugh at the glare he was getting from Elijah. The man was so uptight he'd probably break into a million pieces if he so much as laughed.

"Now, Princess, Uncle Elijah is so excited for you to spend the night. How about this, if Daddy says it's okay, I'll pick you up Friday, and you can hang out with us until he gets off work. Besides, you start school next week."

"Can I wear my new boots?"

"You'll have to ask Daddy about that."

"Okay, but why can't I come with you?"

Trouble almost gave in and told her yes. His strong suit wasn't going to be the strict one; that would have to be Brody's job. Internally he winced at the thoughts going through his head. They were only dating. Right now, Trouble was the cool friend or Uncle. He wasn't her dad, but he wanted to be someday.

"I'm taking your Daddy on a date, just the two of us. You can come next time."

"Promise?"

"Promise."

"Okay, will I see Tank? I've been learning to talk with my hands."

"He'll probably be working, but we'll see."

"Fine," Princess pouted. "You tell him I've been learning."

"I'll tell him." He kissed her cheek and set her on her little biker boot clad feet.

"I have another one to contend with?"

"Tank's awesome! He talks with his hands, and he has this long beard, and he growls like a bear." Princess talked a mile a minute as she walked over to pick up her bag.

"Now I'm supposed to contend with a growly tattooed grizzly bear that has this incredible skill."

"I've got my cards and my movies, we'll practice. He's really good, but Uncle Scary says I'll learn quick. He says I'm super smart."

Trouble watched Elijah roll his eyes and realized the man didn't know how to share his family. He kind of felt sorry for him. He'd had them all to himself for years, and now this huge new group of people comes in. Brody said goodbye and kissed Princess loudly on her cheeks, hugged his brother and showed them out.

"I'm sorry about Elijah."

"It's gotta be a hard thing when she's got a bunch of new people, and he's getting pushed to the side."

"Yeah, he'll get used to it, but it's still new."

"You ready to go?"

"Yeah, where are we going?"

"One of our regulars owns a place called Vincent's, he's also the chef. He's been telling us to come in forever, but—"

"Pizza and beer are easier, then there's the diner."

"Yep, Vincent's sounds a bit fancy, and we don't clean up often."

"I like you in your jeans and t-shirts."

"I like you in anything, well, nothing but a towel is my favorite though."

"Let's go eat."

He knew Brody wasn't ready to take the next step, one that Trouble was almost desperate for, almost a year of abstinence did that to a man. He opened the door and waited for Brody to exit, then he locked and closed it behind him.

"We driving?"

"No, it's in walking distance, I thought it would give us time just to talk."

"Okay."

They turned right at the sidewalk and started down the block. Powers, Georgia wasn't a booming metropolis. It was big enough though.

"Did you ever think about leaving here," Brody asked.

"I did for a while, went to college, but it just wasn't for me. I barely made it through high school." He hated to admit he wasn't the smartest man around. "When I decided that I wanted to work with Gib, I came home. What about you?"

"No, I like it here, and Elijah's here. College would've been great, but there was never a time or money to go. I'd planned to be a teacher."

"What about now that Princess is going to school?"

"Again, it's having the time and money. I've got a job with a regular paycheck that makes the bills, not much more than that."

"You're doing great though." He took Brody's hand and laced their fingers as they crossed over Claremont Street. He didn't like when Brody put himself down. Brody worked hard, Princess was amazing, and Brody was sweet, funny and damn near perfect.

"Thanks, Elijah had to put off school until I was older. Maybe when Mina's older and more independent, I can think about going back. Do you like where you are with your job and all?"

"It's fucking great, meet new people, learn all their stories, hit some conventions a few times a year. Everyone thinks I had a charmed life growing up. The rich kid with all the best shit, but until I met the Phelps family, it wasn't great."

"How did you meet Landon?"

"We met in third grade. He walked right up to me and said we're friends. No asking or nothing. I just went along, but normally that's how it went with him. Landon has some kind of feelings barometer. He can instantly tell your mood from one syllable. I think that's why he picked me.

"Landon was this cool kid. He was nerdy as fuck though and totally out. Even when we were kids, he knew, and he didn't apologize for it. Everyone knew who his Dad was. Everyone was losing their shit over Landon getting a bike for his sixteenth. We all were jealous as hell. We've been best friends our whole lives."

"I think Carla was my best friend and I think that was the problem."

He turned to study Brody's profile, noticed his tensed jaw and a slight frown. Brody didn't talk much about Carla aside from the few questions Trouble had asked when they first started hanging out.

"What do you mean?"

"We were best friends. Inseparable and I think it was just everyone assumed we were dating so we went with it. We both had plans after high school that had us going our separate ways, still friends, but different schools and goals."

"So, marriage wasn't in the cards," he asked as they neared the restaurant and he stopped outside, sitting down on a bench and pulling Brody down with him.

"Shouldn't we go inside?"

"Explain first, plenty of time. So, marriage?"

He didn't care about dinner. The date was about getting to know Brody one-on-one. If Brody wanted, he'd take him to the diner, and they'd pig out on greasy burgers and fries. The location of the date wasn't important to him.

"Definitely not. In hindsight, I think if we had decided not to get married, stay friends and raised Mina things would've been different."

"You can always ask the what-ifs, but what happened, well happened." He stretched his arm along the backrest and relaxed as he waited for Brody to continue.

Brody let out a heavy sigh and leaned back against the bench. "I think it would've ended up the same. Me with Mina and Carla off at college, doing her thing. When we talk it's friendly, but not like when we were in high school and talked for hours about our futures. Besides Elijah, she's the first one I came out to as bisexual. She just smiled and went on like it was just another day."

"I came out early to everyone but my parents, I waited until I was eighteen and on my way out the door. Part of me knew they'd see it as one of my many failings."

"You didn't fail at anything. Your family seems like assholes."

"Public image is a really big thing. Which is weird because my parents' life started as a scandal."

"How so?"

"Well, my Mom's not really from the richest family. Dad and her got drunk one night at college. Nine months later, here I came. They were forced to get married. The stories I heard was his girlfriend was more than a little pissed. I think I reminded them of their fuck up, I was what ruined—"

"You didn't ruin a damn thing and if they're that petty then its best you stay away."

"Brought the mood down, didn't I?"

"Shut up and take me to get something to eat. Chubby guys love their food."

"You're sexy as fuck and don't think differently. You in nothing but that towel has been night and morning jerk off material since I saw it, not that I didn't think about it before."

"You, um—"

"Why do you think I spent a year setting myself up for rejection?"

"Glutton for punishment? Joke on the chubby guy?"

Had Brody thought all his offers of dates were about making fun of him? He shook his head, "You're no joke. I thought you were sexy in this cute, innocent sort of way the first time I saw you. I wanted to muss you. Fuck, I was a fucking goner."

He noticed Brody was turned away, he lifted his hand and pinched Brody's chin to turn Brody to look at him.

"Did I say something wrong?"

"No, it's just, you're gorgeous, and you know that, so don't go denying it. But you're also funny, sweet and so good with Mina. I just—"

"Don't question, don't start doubting shit. It's our first date just us. No one's in a hurry. I like you and Mina. We just do our thing, and it'll work out however it works. You don't want more than friends for now that's fine. I want more, but you have Mina, she comes first. Just don't ask me to back off." He wanted to distract from the heaviness or possible rejection. "I was thinking about getting Princess a sidecar for my bike." He stood as Brody's eyes went round and slightly panicked.

"What the hell are you talking about?"

Brody was close on his heels as he walked through the door.

"Well, she's gotta come on our Sunday runs. I checked the law—"

The debate continued through drink orders, appetizers and halfway through dinner. He knew it was low, but he'd checked into the age minimums and all. She was old enough, and he wanted to take Brody and Mina out on Sundays. He just needed the conversation to go elsewhere. He knew the *let's just be friends* conversation was coming, but he wasn't ready for it. He wasn't willing to give them up yet. It might not be real, but he wanted just a bit longer with the two people he was quickly considering his family.

# 10 FIRST DAY OF SCHOOL

Luckily Mina was still in bed from being too excited to sleep last night. He finished packing her lunch and set it on the table. Time to get the monster up. Brody walked out of the kitchen and was about to head for the hall when the doorbell rang. Who the hell would be here at six-thirty a.m.? He padded to the door and looked through the peephole and groaned as he saw a very excited Lucky on the other side.

He opened the door, and his eyes widened as he noticed the whole crew standing there.

"Good morning, baby," Trouble stepped up, quickly kissed him and walked into the apartment. "Princess up yet? Nope, I wasn't attacked, I'll go wake her up." Trouble jogged toward the hallway and disappeared.

"What's going on?"

"It's Princess's first day of school!" Lucky practically vibrated as he bounced into the house. "I brought her outfits, you don't look like you—"

"Lucky," Scary growled as he pushed Lucky out of the way and entered. "Hey, Brody."

"Hi, Scary. Y'all came for Mina's first day of school?" He didn't know if that was a question or statement. He'd known Trouble would've been there in time to leave, but this was more than he'd thought.

"Would we miss this?" Zerk walked in with Landon under his arm.

Then he noticed it, they all looked exhausted—almost hungover. His apartment had just been descended upon by a wave of hungover locusts.

"Have y'all even been asleep?"

"Yes, but Lucky and Trouble went to Scary's first banging on his door until he got up, then they headed back home to jump all over us—literally." Landon rolled his eyes. "I think they've been trying to stay a few steps ahead of Scary since they left his house."

He could see that Scary didn't look friendly on a regular day, but he ran a bar, and he knew how those hours were.

Priest brought up the rear rubbing his fingers through his shaggy, ginger curls. "You okay, Priest?"

"I was accosted at five a.m. by a hyper hippie, how would you feel?"

He couldn't help laughing at Priest's exasperated tone, and then Priest was attacked again by said hyper hippie.

"I've gotta do hair and dress the Princess," Lucky practically squealed and ran off.

"You'd think it was his first day of school. I've spent more time in fabric warehouses this past week than I ever want to see again. He's been sewing like crazy. Princess has a whole new wardrobe."

"He made her a whole—"

He couldn't even finish the question. Tears began to gather at the corner of his eyes, and suddenly strong thick arms enveloped him.

"Hey, none of that. Got coffee," Zerk asked before wandering off.

"I better go and make sure she's up." He turned away quickly and made his way to Mina's room. He found Trouble sitting on the side of her tiny bed while Trouble watched her with a serene expression. Lucky wasn't as calm since he was bouncing on his toes nervously as Mina took in outfit after outfit being held up.

His daughter appeared as overwhelmed by these men as he was. Their generosity and obvious love for his daughter amazed him. Their little family expanded in such a short time.

"We have an hour to get her dressed and to school," he said from the doorway.

"Daddy, did you see?"

"Yes, did you say—"

"Yes, I said thank you. Uncle Lucky made me all these pretty clothes. He said he'd teach me."

"That's very nice, let's get your teeth brushed and your hair—"

"I've got hair and clothes. You just get the rest. I got this," Lucky said as he critically studied the clothes that looked like the sixties exploded. Lucky seemed to make a decision and went to hang up the other clothes.

He held out his hand to Mina, and she came to him. He took her to get ready but also to give him a minute to adjust and his mind around all this. It was too much too early in the morning.

◆ ◆ ◆

He was about to lose his mind. Mina was situated in a sidecar in a teal blue that perfectly matched Trouble's bike. A helmet on her messy mop of curls and braids Lucky had done with superhuman speed. There were bikes behind and in front of him as they all drove to Mina's school. He could only imagine what they looked like pulling up. Huge, tattooed men on motorcycles in leather escorting a tiny hippie in training to Kindergarten.

They pulled up, and they backed up to the curb almost as a single mind. Parking and turning off the engines in unison. Mina was right in the middle of it. Trouble's leather jacket wrapped around the cream-colored two-piece outfit. He was still amazed by the craftsmanship.

He parked his vehicle and groaned as he saw Elijah running across the street.

"What the hell is going on?"

Elijah cussing even hell was almost unheard of, but there it was. "The guys showed up this morning to escort her to school."

"I can see that."

He followed Elijah's gaze to where Trouble was taking off her helmet. Trouble lifted Mina from the sidecar and then removed the leather jacket.

"Wow, where did you get those clothes, they're beautiful."

"Lucky made them plus several others. Apparently, he thought my fashion sense wouldn't encourage enough individuality and self-expression."

"You have weird friends."

"I do. I'm still a bit overwhelmed by what they all did."

"I'm not exactly used to them and probably never will be, but they treat you and Mina amazingly."

"They do, especially Trouble. I don't—"

"Don't question it. Just enjoy it. You're very lucky."

Something in Elijah's voice made him jerked his gaze to his brother. There was a hint of sadness in Elijah's eyes. He'd never quite seen his brother look that way. Elijah gave up a lot to raise him. Postponed college, and in some ways Elijah was postponing his whole life, or he was stuck in a permanent loop he couldn't break free from. He knew Elijah hadn't gone on a date in a year or more. Suddenly he felt like a selfish shit and wondered how much Elijah had missed out on being essentially a father since their parents had brought him home. He didn't even have any faded memories of his parents ever doing anything with him. It had always been Elijah. He suddenly wrapped his arms around Elijah and hugged him tightly.

"What—"

"Thank you."

"For what?"

"Everything, you were the best Dad a little shit like me could've had."

He had heard Elijah's faint sniffle before the older man pulled away. "Stop making any more of a spectacle of yourself than you already have. We already have a huge audience."

He turned to find most of the parents and kids outside the school staring at them. All he could do was smile. He shook his head and walked toward Mina standing with the guys in a protective half-circle behind her. She had a rainbow backpack slung over her shoulders with peace signs hanging from the zippers.

"Are you ready," he asked as he crouched down beside her.

"No, I wanna go home."

"Hey..." Trouble mirrored him on the other side. "You're gonna do great. You're gonna make a bunch of friends. You're already the coolest kid walking through that door."

Mina threw her arms around Trouble's neck and held on tight as the man cuddled her to his chest. Then Mina was in his arms.

"Tell your Uncles bye so we can go in and get you settled."

"Can they come in with us?"

"I think it's only parents."

"Then Trouble can come." Mina turned and hugged each of the crew and Elijah, each one giving her words of encouragement.

It didn't escape his attention that she'd lumped Trouble in the parent category and he wasn't quite sure how he felt about that. Hell, he didn't know how Trouble felt about it. Before he had time to question it, Mina grabbed onto his and Trouble's hands checked both ways, then dragged them across the street.

It seemed forever to get her settled into the classroom. She held onto both their hands and didn't want to let go. His baby was starting school. He still remembered the day he'd brought her home from the hospital and the long months of no sleep. The first time she said Daddy still played in his mind.

"Mr. Vaughn, she'll be fine, all the parents have a hard time the first day." A beautiful, blonde with a bright, friendly smile who introduced herself as Ms. Noah assured him.

They stepped out into the hall as Mina started to stow her bag into a cubby with her name on it.

"I know, but she was nervous. It was nice to meet you, Ms. Noah."

"You as well, but before you go, where did you get Mina's outfit? It's amazing, and my daughter would love it."

"Her Uncle Lucky made it for her."

"That's handmade?"

"Yeah, he's spent the past week making her a new wardrobe. He's been driving us crazy with fabric samples," Trouble groaned.

He didn't know if he liked the teacher eyeing Trouble like she was. He wasn't accustomed to jealousy, and he didn't like it at all.

"Maybe I could get his number. Ask him about making a few things for her birthday."

"Just call Twirled World Ink and ask for Lucky, he's there most days."

"Thanks, I better get back to them." She said her goodbyes and returned to the classroom.

"You ready to go, it's almost time for you to head to work."

"Yeah, but we need to stop by the office first."

"Okay, you want me to wait outside until you're done?"

"No."

He walked the empty halls toward the office, then he walked through the propped open door.

"Hi, I'm Brody Vaughn, Mina Vaughn's dad, I needed to add someone to her approved emergency contact and pick up list."

"Of course, here's the paperwork. We'll add it to her file."

"Maybe I should ask first if you want—"

"Fill it out."

Trouble whispered it, but he had a feeling if they weren't in public he would have yelled it. Trouble shoved his hands in his pockets and rocked back on his heels. A panicked look on his face as if Brody didn't fill it out in the next thirty seconds he'd change his mind. To Mina and him, Trouble became important to their lives. He hadn't realized the full extent until that morning. He wanted to keep Trouble around. The future wasn't a guarantee, but he was tired of holding back and denying his growing feelings for Trouble. The man and his off-the-wall family had somehow become his without him noticing. Trouble and the Twirled Crew were exactly what Mina and he needed.

# 11 ATTACK OF THE SADISTIC FAMILY

A mid-week afternoon rush was unheard of, but they'd slammed him for the last two hours. He was already exhausted. He hadn't been sleeping well and then getting Mina and him ready in the morning made that worse. The new schedule was taking some getting used to, and he knew it would take time, but he was frustrated. He was also frustrated in more ways than one. Trouble had stopped by a few nights over the week, but he hadn't stayed the night again. Trouble's touches and kisses were innocent and maddeningly platonic. He'd waited for it to happen. He'd rather have Trouble as a friend than nothing at all. No, that wasn't true, he wanted more than friends.

He was tired of laying in his empty bed at night with only his hand and fantasies of Trouble for relief. His sex drive had been muted over the years. Yes, he stroked one out when he needed to relieve tension, but his masturbation sessions were turning into nightly, unsatisfying sessions.

Now was not the time to think about it. He didn't know how to broach the subject. What if Trouble did just want to be friends and he completely embarrassed himself by asking only to be turned down? He groaned as he took the disinfectant cleaner and started wiping down all the belts, scanners and card readers. There was only another hour on his shift then it would be time to go pick up Mina. He was going to have to have Lucky teach him to do Mina's hair because apparently, he didn't do it right.

"Excuse me?"

A cold, clipped voice caused him to turn. With years of practice and experience, he plastered on a friendly smile as he sensed this was going to be a pain in the ass customer.

"Yes, ma'am, how can I help you today?" There was something familiar about the perfectly done blonde hair, and in the shape of the ice blue eyes, they were Trouble's eyes. Except these were cold and filled with disgust and didn't have laugh lines, the woman was botoxed to the point of expressionless.

"Are you Brody Vaughn?"

"Yes, do I know you."

"I need you to stay away from my son. He isn't all that bright. Damaged since I was made to give—"

"Ma'am, I apologize for interrupting you, but I don't think this is the proper place." He applauded himself for keeping his rage under control. Trouble wasn't damaged or dumb, he was beautiful and kind.

"I'm only going to warn you once, and this is it. You don't leave my son alone, I'll make sure your lowly existence will get even lower. We're tired of ignoring the embarrassment—"

"I think its time for you go."

"Brody, is everything okay?"

Relief swamped him at his boss' voice, and he turned to give him a reassuring smile.

"Yes, sir, Mrs. Carver was just leaving." He turned back to the woman, and the disgust morphed into something darker. "Good day, Mrs. Carver."

"This isn't over, young man, you do have a young daughter to consider. Do you want her around those deviants?"

"My daughter loves her Uncles and Trouble, and they love her. I would think twice about threatening her."

"Ma'am, I think Brody said you were just leaving." He'd never heard Stan's voice that cold before.

Mrs. Carver left without another word, but he knew in the pit of his stomach that this wasn't the end and it terrified him how bad it would get.

"Is there something I should keep an eye on?"

"I'm so sorry this won't—"

"Brody, you've worked here for four years, and you're my most reliable employee, everyone, staff and customers love you. Now, I can't help if I'm not warned about trouble. We're a small family-owned store and as my grandfather said when he started this place was always treat your employees like family. So, tell me."

"I've become friends with Trouble."

"I think that's an understatement, my husband goes to Twirled for his ink." Brody tried not to let his mouth fall open at the confession. "Trouble has been asking you out forever. I'm glad to see you finally gave in. He's a very nice young man."

"Yes, he is. That was his mother. His family isn't very nice to him, and she was threatening me to stay away from him."

"Go on and talk to Trouble, I know Mina doesn't get off school for another hour. Don't let this sit. He needs to know."

"I can go after—"

"Would you rather have this conversation in private or with Mina nearby where she can overhear. You can come in early or stay a little later to make up the hour if you want."

"Thank you."

"You're welcome. If she comes in again, please let me know. Also, it might be smart to keep a journal. I've known the Carver family, and the rumors in this town are they all aren't exactly right. The whole bunch is cruel and entitled. Don't worry about your job because I know if it hasn't gone through your head it probably will."

"I appreciate this." Brody stowed the cleaning bottle and paper towels, then grabbed his backpack heading for the door. It was a short walk to the shop, but he didn't want to run late picking Mina up.

He drove quickly and parked beside the long row of bikes in front of Twirled. Luckily, Trouble's was one of them. He got out and headed to the door, as soon as he walked through Trouble looked up with a happy smile. His gorgeous eyes crinkled at the corners.

"Hey, you're early, I thought I'd see you at the house later." Trouble's voice was a smooth baritone.

He loved the sound of it. He lifted his hand to rub at the back of his neck. It felt like he was being watched, but he knew he was just paranoid.

"Can I talk to you?"

"Sure." Trouble's voice lost its happiness, and that killed him. "We can go in the back."

He followed behind Trouble taking in the width of his broad shoulders and the way his body formed a V down to a trim waist, he also had a great ass. So not the appropriate thoughts right then. Trouble opened the door and stepped back to let him go first. Trouble was the first to speak when the door closed.

"Did I do something wrong?" The question sounded so sad and broken.

"No, you didn't do anything. Your mother came to the store just now."

"Oh." It didn't sound like a surprised noise.

"You knew she would."

"She's done it before. I like someone, and she threatens them, offers them money and they go away. I try not to like anyone."

Trouble widened the distance between them, and he didn't like it at all. It was as if the man was already giving up.

"Trouble, what does that mean?"

"I hook up, it isn't the greatest, and I feel like shit the next morning, but it's something, ya know."

"Have you since—"

Trouble's eyes went wide, and he vehemently shook his head. "No, only you, I haven't seen anyone since I started asking you out. I ain't like that."

"I didn't think you were, I'm sorry, she has my head all screwed up."

"Did she threaten Princess? I can stay away, she's more important than anything."

Trouble dropped his chin to his chest and shoved his hands into the pockets of his threadbare jeans. His t-shirt pulled tight against the powerful mounds of his chest muscles.

"Did she mess up your job?"

"No, the owner was there, and he overheard everything, and he told me not to worry about my job. Stan's husband comes here for his ink."

"Garnet's great. Likes bold and abstract, you can really go crazy with his designs."

"What are we going to do about your mother?"

"Do you want me to go away? I mean we haven't really…I like you a lot, and I love Mina. It's like having a family all my own, but I won't have that threatened."

"You'd give us up to protect us?"

"It would break my heart, but yes."

He couldn't take the way his happy and beautiful Trouble was pulled into himself, sacrificing his happiness so he and Mina could be safe. He closed the few feet that separated them. Trouble kept his hands in his pockets but noticed he fisted them in the confines of the denim. Lifting his hands, he cupped Trouble's face and tugged him down. He hesitated when their mouths barely touched.

"I despise the fact she thinks she can get her way by threatening Mina, but Mina is ours. She loves you as much as you love her. We wouldn't know what to do without you, so no talk about disappearing on us. Got it."

"Yes." Trouble lifted his chin, so their lips brushed.

"You gonna kiss me like you mean it," he inquired and grinned as he retreated as Trouble tried to kiss him. "You've been keeping a lot of distance the past few weeks. I didn't like it."

"You didn't? Missed me?" Trouble's hands gripped his sides tightly as his thumbs stroked the curve of his belly.

He moaned and nodded his head.

"I've been trying to be good." Trouble's mouth slanted over his, sharp, fleeting nipping kisses stung his lips as Trouble brought their bodies together.

He laid his arms over Trouble's shoulders and played with the dark blond hair at his nape. It was soft and tickled his palms. He could barely breathe, it had been so long since Trouble had held him, the quick hugs recently weren't enough.

"Why have you been trying to be good?" His voice was a rough whisper.

"I wanted you to know you were special and real—mine."

That's when the kiss went from teasing to rough and deep. Trouble's tongue fucked his mouth in rough strokes. Trouble hands gripped his hips and tugged him forward, and the big man's hard dick sunk into the softness of his belly. He didn't even think about sucking it in because Trouble's hips stuttered as he ground into him. He loved that Trouble had a thing about his soft, rounded stomach especially by the large and incredibly ripped Trouble.

"Fuck, I love how soft you are, perfect just for me—"

Trouble's growled words turned into a deep rumble in his chest as Trouble kissed him once more and pulled away but didn't separate their bodies.

"This is why I was trying to be good. I've wanted you for months, and then you let me sleep with you. Every night I have to fucking jerk off thinking about spreading your thighs and claiming that ass." A soft kiss brushed his lips. "But once I do, I'm never letting you go."

Brody was turned on; he swore his boxer briefs were wet from pre-come leaking out with every pulse of his cock.

"Come over tonight, spend the night."

"Are you sure?"

"Yes, I've been sure, but afraid."

"Afraid?"

"That you weren't real. You're so sweet, and you think about Mina and me before you think of yourself. You made her first day of school amazing with the help of your friends. When you don't come over in the evenings, you still call to tell her and me good night. I've wanted to say yes to you since the first time you asked me out, but—"

"But what? Don't bullshit just tell me."

"You're so fucking gorgeous, and I'm—"

"Mine, I said you're mine."

"So tonight, after work, my place?"

"I'll be done around six, I wanna read Princess her bedtime story. She asked me the other night, but I had a late appointment and couldn't come over."

"Fine, we'll make you dinner and Mina got a new movie she's been wanting to watch but only when you come over."

"Is it the Dragon one?"

For a huge bad ass, he was cute, but he'd heard Lucky and Trouble were cartoon fanatics. If it was animated and funny, they were all over it. "Yes, the second one."

"I'll try to finish up early."

"I better go get Mina from school. Don't want to be late."

"No, she gets anxious when it gets close to the time you're supposed to be there. I hate she thinks someone's going to forget her."

Trouble had picked Mina up a few days when he got stuck at work waiting for a replacement to show. He kissed Trouble once more and stepped away. Some of the happiness seemed to drain away when their bodies separated, and there was space between them again. He wanted to know why. He hadn't wanted to ask about what his family life was like before, but now that it intruded on their life, he needed to know.

They'd talk later after Mina went to bed and then he'd finally have Trouble in his bed again. He was nervous as hell, but he wasn't going to give Trouble up for anything—not even for Trouble to be selfless and sacrifice himself for others. He just wondered how many times in the past he'd had to do it, destroy himself to save another. He had a feeling he wasn't going to like the answer.

# 12 WALKING THROUGH HELL WITH HEAVEN ON THE OTHER SIDE

Trouble finished up in record time and headed home to pack a few things to crash at Brody's. He hadn't been this nervous about a sleepover with a man since he'd lost his virginity Freshman year in college. Even that didn't come close to what he felt now.

It didn't help his mom was trying to ruin shit like she always did. The threat would happen first, then the bribe. None of his past boyfriends made it passed the offer of money. He found they replaced him easy enough, and he didn't want to think Brody would go the way of the others, but he cared way too much. Tonight wasn't about his mom's bullshit or his exes. It was about time with Brody and Mina.

He parked beside Brody's car, quickly gathered his stuff and exited his truck, locking and closing the door behind him. As always, the door opened before he got to it and Brody waited for him with a sweet, welcoming smile. He dropped his gaze to Mina who appeared and leaned against Brody's leg.

"Hey, thought you'd be at the shop another hour."

"Finished up early and told the guys I was headed out." He lowered his head and kissed Brody, the man's soft lips conformed to his, and he instantly wanted more. "Hey, Princess." He swept her into his arms and kissed her cheek loudly making her giggle.

"Hi, Trouble." Princess squeezed his neck tight.

"Come on you two, we need to finish up dinner."

Brody placed his hand on Trouble's lower back. He walked inside, setting his bag and Princess down. He loved that Brody touched him. Before Brody, he couldn't remember the last man who touched him without it being a prelude to sex. He worried about his control, a year past since he'd given into his urges for a comfort fuck and that's all they were. A momentary need to be wanted no matter how brief.

"Quit thinking so much." Brody's soft lips caressed his ear as Brody whispered in his ear.

"Landon says I do it a lot, I never noticed."

"Well, Landon's right." Brody bent over and picked up his bag. "I'm going to put this in the bedroom, and I'll meet you in the kitchen."

"Okay, what do you need me to do?"

"I haven't figured out what to make for dinner. I was getting ready to check."

"Princess and I will check out the options."

"I've heard the horror stories, don't even think about starting anything."

"Wasn't planning on it, I'd rather not spend tonight in the hospital for food poisoning."

Brody barked out a laugh and strode in the direction of the bedrooms, he watched until Brody disappeared.

"Let's go see what Daddy has to make for dinner."

"I want noodles."

"We'll check to see if we have noodles." If they didn't, he'd get some. He found he liked taking care of Brody and Princess.

He took her hand and let her lead him to the kitchen with her talking a mile a minute. She caught him up on school and her ASL lessons, the teachers thought it was great she was learning on her own. She'd apparently told them all about her Uncle Tank. While she continued to talk, he found noodles and a jar of sauce in Brody's pantry.

He set both items on the counter and opened the fridge, there was juice boxes, sodas, and chocolate milk, which was Brody's weakness.

"Can I have a juice box please?"

"Sure." He grabbed one and turned around to hand it to Princess.

"Thank you." She took it and worked to get the straw into the hole.

"Figure out what's for dinner?"

"Princess wanted noodles. I found what I thought she'd like."

"I know it isn't anything fancy." Brody seemed embarrassed.

"What's wrong?"

"Nothing, there's just not a lot to choose from, and I'm sure—"

"Stop, I ain't got a problem with any of this. I'm not here because of what you got. I love time with you and Princess."

"Okay, I better get dinner started."

"Can I help?"

"No, just sit over there, I got this." Brody walked toward him and nudged him toward the table to sit with Mina.

He liked this, and he didn't want it to go away, all he had to do was figure out how to get his parents to back off. Advice is what he needed, who could he talk to though? Gib and Peaches treated him like a son, the way he thought his real parents should have treated him. All he could do was be patient.

♦ ♦ ♦

He leaned back against the wall opposite Mina's room. Brody was just pulling the door shut, but left it slightly ajar. The man increasingly grew nervous as the night wore on and he didn't like it. He didn't want Brody to be apprehensive about anything that happened or didn't between them.

His dick was having a war with his brain. A year of buildup and sexual frustration threatened to completely fry the small amount of functioning brain cells he possessed.

"C'mere." Trouble shoved his hands into his pockets at Brody's expression. "Did I do something to make you nervous around me? I thought—"

"No, it's nothing like that," Brody answered and closed the distance between their bodies. Brody tilted his head back to meet his gaze.

"Then what is it," he asked as he closed his arms around Brody.

"I haven't dated at all since my divorce."

"Having Princess probably made it difficult." He hesitated as he lowered his mouth to press to Brody's for a brief kiss.

"It's not that either, dating meant someone we'd get attached to, and they'd eventually leave."

"So, you think I'm going to leave?"

Brody dropped his forehead to his chest and exhaled heavily sending a warm rush of air across his skin through his t-shirt. He kneaded the small of Brody's back.

"I don't know how to do this."

Brody slipped his hands beneath Trouble's shirt and stroked along his sides then to his abs. At the hesitant touch, he tightened his stomach.

"Carla and me...I've only ever been with her, and it's been so long."

"Nothing has to happen. I ain't gonna lie and say I don't want to, but I can wait."

Brody seemed to be thinking it over and the more time dragged out he figured he had his answer.

"Want to go watch—"

Brody hooked his hands in his waistband and tugged him toward the bedroom.

"I didn't say I didn't want to, I'm just—" Brody backed into the bedroom. "You're the second person I've ever been interested in. Maybe, kind of a big deal. Close the door."

He resisted the urge to kick it closed. Brody reached for the bottom of his t-shirt, and the man's natural shyness caused him to freeze. He didn't want Brody to be self-conscious with him. Every inch of Brody was perfect to him.

"Please," he pleaded. He'd beg to be able to see all of his man.

His cock gave a pleasurable jerk behind his zipper as Brody exposed pale, smooth skin, and the roundness of his stomach. Brody's softness drove him toward uncontrollable need. Brody's soft features pinked as he removed the shirt over his head.

"Why aren't you getting undressed?"

He didn't answer merely ripped his t-shirt over his head and tossed it aside. He'd taken off his socks and boots earlier in the night, so all that remained were his jeans and boxer briefs. In minutes, he was naked in front of Brody, and he couldn't help smirking at his rounded eyes. He encircled his dick and gave the thick length a few quick pumps. His muscles bunched and released at the lust turning his blood hot. The cool air of the bedroom and pleasure caused him to tremble as sweat dampened his body.

"You're still dressed."

"I think I should put my shirt back on."

No, that shit wasn't happening, Brody wasn't going to hide from him. He released his cock and reached Brody in two long strides. "I've seen you in nothing but a towel. Fuck, I love what I saw," he growled as he lifted his hands to cup Brody's face. "Beautiful. Handsome. Mine." He nipped Brody's lips between each word, then he fell to his knees, he kissed across Brody's soft stomach, tongued the shallow indent of his navel.

"You can't—"

Whatever Brody was going to say ended on a moan as he nuzzled Brody's cock through the soft cotton of his sleep pants.

"Oh, I so fucking can."

He didn't waste time or give Brody another second to be shy, he fisted the cotton and tugged it down Brody's legs. "Step out."

Brody obeyed and lifted each foot. He pressed his nose to the curls at the base of Brody's cock and inhaled. He teased Brody's hard dick with his stubble. Brody groaned, and slender fingers combed through his hair. Brody's blunt nails scored his scalp. He sat back on his heels and tilted his head back to take in Brody's flushed face.

He pulled Brody down to straddle his thighs, and without further thought, they tenderly explored each other. They learned the textures of skin, scars and hair. Kissed in long, unhurried minutes, but could've been hours. He'd never wanted to be gentle—to love on someone for hours. He wanted to come, to lose himself in Brody, but he savored each moan and shiver. His name was a lust-filled rumbling whisper repeated against his mouth.

Sitting back and crossed his legs, he settled Brody in the cradle of his thighs. Brody dick jerked and left smears of pre-come in the hair on Trouble's belly. He wrapped his hand around both hard shafts and stroked his thumb over the heads, gathering the drops then slowly began to pump. He kept his eyes on Brody's.

"Don't close them, I wanna see when you fucking lose it for me."

"We're not—"

"Penetration isn't the only way I can love you." He bit Brody's plump bottom lip, and he spoke around the captured flesh. "We have all—"

Their breathing became labored, and Brody touched him wherever he could reach. Kisses, grunts and groans, he stopped pumping long enough to spit into his hand then go back to working their dicks in quick, rough movements.

He felt the pulsing of Brody's cock, heard the catch in his breath seconds before jets of come sprayed across his stomach. That's all it took, one, two, three more strokes and he slammed his mouth onto Brody's, thrusting his tongue deep as he emptied his balls, his come joining Brody's.

He eased the kiss and rested their foreheads together, looked between their bodies. He rubbed their combined release into the curve of Brody's belly and loving the give. Several minutes passed in silence and he leaned his body backward far enough to see Brody's eyes closed, his lashes damp.

"What's this," he asked as he leaned in and brushed his lips to Brody's eyes. Did he do something wrong? What if he pushed Brody too fast and his man regretted it? He suddenly felt his chest tightening with an anxiety attack he hadn't had in years.

"Thank you, I'm just, I don't know." Brody opened his eyes and smiled.

That curve of Brody's lush lips eased the vice around his chest.

"Want to take a shower?"

"Yeah, we're a little sticky."

"Get used to it. We're gonna do this a lot."

"Is that right?"

"Yep." He kissed him one more time. "Get up, we'll go take a shower, then bedtime. I know you have work in the morning." He wondered if one day they'd be able to spend a whole day in bed. Maybe he could talk to the guys or Elijah to see if they'd babysit Princess.

"No killing my alarm in the morning."

"No promises, six a.m. is cruel and unusual punishment."

He loved the sound of Brody's laugh. Hell, he just loved the man. At the thought, the panic was back. What if Brody never loved him? Found him lacking like everyone else. He knew, unlike the times before Brody, leaving him would destroy him.

He helped Brody stand and steady him before he got to his own feet. They dressed in pajama bottoms and exited the bedroom. He wanted—no needed more nights like that. He closed the bathroom door behind them. He had to make sure Brody never had a reason to turn him away, but fucking up terrified him. Pushing the thoughts aside he joined Brody under the shower spray. He memorized every moment in case he needed them in a lonely future. A future he wasn't so sure he'd have.

# 13 HE SHOULD'VE HEEDED THE WARNING

He barely held back tears as a social worker walked through his house. She'd arrived ten minutes after he'd gotten home from work and was just getting caught up on Mina's day. They'd received an anonymous report of neglect and child endangerment. He knew who made that fucking call.

"Who watches your daughter when you work evenings?"

"Either my brother Elijah Vaughn—"

"Mayor Vaughn?"

"Yes, ma'am, but I don't work many evenings—"

A knock cut him off, and he turned to open the door, when it opened, he found Peaches. He didn't understand why one of Trouble's bosses was there and dressed like she was going to court. She had on an expensive looking suit which hid most of her tattoos which were a feat in and of itself.

"Oh, honey, I got here as fast as possible." He was enveloped in a tight embrace.

"Grandma," Mina came running in and wrapped herself around Peaches' legs.

"How's my sweet girl," Peaches asked as she swung Mina onto her hip.

Okay, his life was getting even more surreal. Mina spent a lot of time with the Twirled Crew, and she'd mentioned Peaches a time or two, but when had his daughter acquired a grandmother?

"I'm Veronica Phelps." Her voice was cold and professional as she introduced herself to the social worker.

"I'm Mrs. Klein with Social Services."

"And I'm Mrs. Phelps, Mr. Vaughn's attorney."

"I don't think this requires a lawyer."

"I'm sure it doesn't, but as this involves my future son-in-law and granddaughter, we'll err on the side of caution. Now, Mrs. Klein, what brings you to my client's home today?"

"We received an anonymous report yesterday about child endangerment and neglect."

"I was informed and have taken a statement that my client was threatened by one Mrs. Carver, the mother of Mr. Vaughn's partner. Have you found any evidence of neglect?"

Brody could only stand by as Peaches worked as if Mina wasn't on her hip with her little face in the crook of her neck. He couldn't get passed the words son-in-law, partner, was that what everyone thought—was that what Trouble thought? He hadn't even dreamed of thinking passed any current moment.

"I just finished the walkthrough and was going to ask Mr. Vaughn some questions."

"By all means, let's go have a seat. Do you have any coffee, Brody?"

"Yes, ma'am, I think Mina went to—"

"I'll lay her down, which way is her room?"

He pointed toward the hallway and Peaches walked away without another word. He was still on the verge of panic and a good cry. Brody wanted Trouble, but in his gut, he had a feeling they were keeping him away. There was one thing he was certain about—Trouble would be torturing himself with guilt.

"Come on in the kitchen, Mrs. Klein."

He strode in the direction of the kitchen and busied himself making coffee. Brody tried to remember if he'd gotten milk or creamer the last time he went grocery shopping.

"So, let's get the Q and A over with, Brody is joining us for family dinner tonight." Peaches breezed into the room.

"You said you don't work a lot of evenings." The woman sat down at the table and opened the leather binder she'd used to take notes since she showed up.

Brody poured three mugs of coffee and noticed Peaches putting milk and sugar on the table.

"No, I have seniority at work, I do work alternating weekends. Mina sometimes spends the night with my brother, or she goes to Jimmy's." It felt unnatural to use Trouble's given name. "And him and his friends watch her."

"Have you been dating Mr. Carver long," Mrs. Klein asked as she doctored her coffee.

"A few months, but we've known each other for a year. We met when Jimmy came into the store where I work."

"Are Mina and him close?"

"She loves him. He always makes sure to call every night to say goodnight to her and find out about her day when he can't come over."

"Mr. Vaughn, I'm going to be honest, in the short time I spent with Mina I've learned she's a very smart and happy child, but unfortunately we do get false reports which make our heavy caseloads even more oppressive, yet we have to take each case seriously."

"I understand that."

"Where is Mina's mother?"

"Carla is an addict, she's in and out of rehab, last I heard she was out and staying with friends."

"Does she have contact with Mina?"

"No, ma'am, when the divorce became final, I was granted full custody. Carla wasn't and isn't in a place where she can care for Mina. Her maternal grandparents also have no contact."

"So, you're her sole guardian?"

"I did have papers drawn up giving Elijah custody in the event something happens to me."

"Wouldn't Mr. Carver like custody?"

"I'm not sure we're at that point yet. He loves her as much as she loves him. They're inseparable when they're together. I'm getting ganged up on by the two of them saying it's time to get her ears pierced, but not stretched like his, I'm not ready for that." He cussed himself for rambling but noticed Mrs. Klein had a slight smile before she hid it.

"Why do you think someone filed a report against you?"

"I don't know. The only issue I've had recently was Mrs. Carver coming by my work to threaten me. She said they wouldn't tolerate the embarrassment of their son's behavior.

"We don't have much, Mrs. Klein, but Mina is fed, warm and loved. She's doing well in school. I'd never do anything to endanger her. It's one of the reasons I haven't dated until now, I didn't want her to become attached to anyone."

Peaches touched his forearm and gave it a squeeze. He turned to find her watching him with an odd expression he recognized as one she gave every member of the crew including Scary. It was what he assumed motherly affection looked like.

"Mrs. Klein, from this moment on we will be recording any suspicious occurrences. If it's found out that Mrs. Carver is harassing Mr. Vaughn, we will be filing for a restraining order."

"After taking a look around, I can see your home is clean and safe. Mina is well-adjusted and doesn't have any appearance of being neglected. I will file my report as this was a false allegation."

Relief swamped him and he sagged as his muscles relaxed, the urge to cry was back though. "Thank you, Mrs. Klein."

"You're welcome, I offer my apologies, but again we have to take every allegation seriously."

Brody nodded and held tight to Peaches' fingers that twined with his.

"But please take your attorney's advice and make sure to keep a record of anything strange no matter how small or innocent it may appear."

"I will."

Mrs. Klein closed and zipped her binder, then stood. He and Peaches did as well, he showed the social worker to the door while Peaches remained behind. He thanked her again and said goodbye. Quickly he returned to the kitchen.

"A lawyer?"

"With my adopted sons, my degree comes in extremely handy although I don't practice anymore, I still keep everything up to date. Are you okay?"

"Yeah, more importantly, is Trouble okay?"

"He's losing his shit, and the boys are gonna hogtie him pretty soon. Trouble may not understand why we kept him away, but—"

"He's going to try to break up with me."

"Brody," Peaches said his name and stepped forward to take his hands. "Listen, Gib and me have known Trouble most of his life, since him and Landon became friends. The Carvers are narcissistic sociopaths, every one of them, who they can't control they attempt to destroy. The guys don't know how he grew up and that's something he doesn't want to share."

"He went to their house for dinner recently."

"Really?"

"Yeah, we texted him thinking he was at work to invite him over for dinner. He called me, and he was crying, he said they hated him."

"I wouldn't be surprised. Trouble was the reason they had to get married, and they've never let him forget how he supposedly ruined their lives."

"I want to see Trouble."

"Pack you and Mina an overnight bag, maybe a few days' worth. Gib's at Twirled House with the grill heating up, we made up one of the empty rooms for Mina to sleep in next to Trouble's. I think a night away would do you good."

He could only nod, and then he was off to pack, taking Peaches' suggestion and packed for a few days. He made sure to grab Mina's backpack and her school clothes. Brody stood beside her bed staring down at her. Part of him wanted to take her and run, but the other, the stronger part couldn't separate them from Trouble. It was early days yet, but he knew what he wanted, and he was prepared to do something completely out of character. He was going to fight for them no matter how nasty it got because his little family was worth it. Every crazy one of them. Although a bigger battle of making sure Trouble didn't try to sacrifice himself for them awaited.

✦✦✦

Chaos reigned as soon as he walked through the front door of Twirled House. They'd lavished so much attention on Mina she'd practically went to sleep sitting up watching her pre-bedtime movie. Trouble had taken her for a ride in her sidecar for a good hour. He'd wanted to protest, but he was starting to recognize the misery in Trouble's gaze which everyone else seemed incapable of noticing. They'd have plenty of time to talk when everyone crashed out for the night.

Finally, Mina was tucked into a huge, king-sized bed, a night light made the mirrored pieces on the upholstered ceiling twinkle like stars. He knew it was Lucky's handy work. The man was a whiz with a sewing machine. He'd never have thought it. After kissing Mina's forehead, he backed out of the room and left the door open. It was Mina's room when she stayed over, so he didn't have to worry about her waking up and not knowing where she was.

He walked to the room next door, entered Trouble's room and closed the door behind him. Brody leaned back against it as he watched Trouble reclined against the headboard. Trouble's hand quickly moved as he worked in his sketchpad. The man never went anywhere without one.

"What'cha working on?"

"Just sketching."

Trouble lied to him. "Are we going to start off the night with a lie?" He approached the bed and crawled onto it, he laid down beside Trouble, but didn't look at the pad.

"It's something for you, but—"

"But what," he asked staring at the ceiling.

"Gib and Peaches have a tradition I always thought was cool, Zerk carried it on with Landon too."

"What it is?"

"Gib tattoos Peaches every year on their anniversary. Designs all his own with meaning for just to the two of them. It's like every year told in ink."

"No wonder she has so many. And what does that have to do with that?" He pointed to the pad.

"It's stupid."

"You've got to stop that. You're not stupid, that's what they always called you, and it's not true."

"I shouldn't keep seeing you or spending time with Mina, I'm like a fucking bad omen."

He rolled to his side and slung his arm across Trouble's stomach to press his body completely to Trouble. "You're not breaking up with me because your mother happens to be an entitled sociopath. The social worker figured out it was a false report. It's done."

"It's not done, she'll keep coming at us until she drives you away."

"Not happening. Now tell me what the sketch is?"

"I'm still working on it. I wanted to give you something for our one year anniversary. I know it's a long time away and you'll probably be sick—"

"Shut up, will you show me when you're done?"

"Yeah, normally Gib makes Peaches wait until the actual day. I don't know if I can be that patient though."

"Me either, I mean my first ink."

"I'm so sorry for what she did." Trouble turned suddenly and buried his face against Brody's chest.

The strength of his hold restricted his breathing. Trouble had tried to squish Mina earlier; she'd giggled and just hugged him back.

"Don't be, it isn't your fault." He stroked Trouble's bare back in soothing circles, and his heart broke as he felt tears wetting his skin.

Trouble cried silently, his body subtly shaking with his sobs, but he made no noises as if he'd had to hide it before. To disguise what his family would consider a weakness. He didn't bring attention to it, he just held him and let him cry. They seemed to lie there forever, then he realized Trouble wasn't shaking. His breathing had evened out, and he'd fallen asleep. He just held him and kissed his soft hair. How much had Trouble suffered growing up keeping it all to himself? To always put himself down—to put himself last?

Brody knew he would do everything to make sure Trouble knew he was loved. First, they had to get passed the newest hurdle—getting Trouble's parents out of their lives. Peaches was on the case; he'd leave that in her capable hands. His job was to keep his family happy, and that's just what the hell he'd do.

# 14 STRATEGY MEETING

The label of his beer slowly peeled back as he steadily picked at it. Mina was off with Peaches while he and Brody met with the guys. He was getting pissed off glares in varying degrees. They'd all known he didn't fuck with his family, but he'd never told them why. Mainly for that reason, he could deal with his annoyed and mad friends but the one thing he couldn't deal with though was the pity.

"You gonna sit there just peeling that label or are ya gonna open your fucking mouth and tell us what this bullshit is," Scary growled from the opposite side of the bar. His huge hands splayed on the surface.

"My family hates me."

"Enough to threaten our Princess?" Lucky sounded appalled.

"My parents had to get married because of me. Dad had to marry her because she got pregnant, Mother ruined his life, so he's bitter and miserable which makes her unhappy. Since she needs someone to take it out on that would be me."

Brody took one of his hands and twined their fingers together.

"Mrs. Carver came by the store a few weeks ago. Said she wouldn't put up with Trouble embarrassing them. Told me to stop seeing him. The threat was pretty clear."

"They can go fuck themselves. They ain't your family, we are!" Lucky flopped back onto one of Scary's couches to lay his head on Priest's lap.

"We can be each other's alibis, and if that doesn't work, we'll have Peaches defend us. It's been awhile since she's put her degree to use," Zerk suggested as he relaxed in a recliner with Landon on his lap.

"Mom does need the practice." Sweet Landon's smile turned evil.

"We're not going to jail." Priest huffed as he played with Lucky's locs.

"I just want them to leave me, Brody and Mina alone."

"Me and my crew could take care of that. I've been told plenty of times they wouldn't mind going back to jail. It'll be like a fucked up reunion for them." Scary poured shots and lined them up.

He felt his lips pull into a small smile. He loved his friends and their attempt at cheering him up. Brody leaned against his side with his head on his shoulder. He just wanted to go away. It wasn't like he purposely sought them out. Avoiding them became a lost cause when they searched him out just to get some fucking sadistic pleasure in completely tearing him down. He felt guilty as fuck they were going after Brody and Mina though, they were his family—the one he'd always wanted. If he didn't solve this shit, he was going to lose them, and he didn't know if he could survive that.

"Quit thinking that," Brody whispered in his ear. "Neither of us is going anywhere."

He didn't understand how Brody read him so easily. He'd gotten good at hiding his pain, but it never worked with Brody. The thing was, he didn't want to hide—to pretend he was something he wasn't. That isn't how he wanted their life together to be, and he always wanted them to be honest.

The doorbell chimed, and Scary growled, "Who the fuck?"

"Probably Elijah," Brody answered and seemed to retreat as Scary's growl got louder.

"Just what I need more people in my house." Scary huffed as he took off for the steps.

"Scary needs to get laid," Lucky suggested.

"He gets laid plenty, he needs to remember their names." Zerk chuckled.

"Don't let him hear you talking about his sex life, he gets cranky about that shit." Trouble took one of the shots and hissed through his clenched teeth. He preferred beer. The whiskey warmed his stomach and didn't exactly settle well. No more liquor for him.

"What the fuck are you harpies up to?" Scary jogged down the steps.

Elijah followed at a slower pace and looked highly uncomfortable. The guy looked like he'd stepped off the cover of some men's fashion magazine. Did the guy not understand casual wear? The man needed to loosen up.

"Nothing," they all answered at once.

"Bullshit." Scary returned to his spot behind the bar. "Beer, shot," he asked Elijah then took his shot followed by two more.

"No thank you, so I received a cryptic text summons, anyone care to enlighten me? With the amount of beer bottles and shot glasses am I safe in assuming I won't like it?"

"Trouble's parents are sociopaths, his mother threatened Brody at work, and then a fucking anonymous report was made to social services," Scary answered without looking up from the next round of shots he was setting up.

"Are you kidding me," Elijah's voice rose a few octaves. "Why didn't you call me?"

"I didn't have a chance. I texted Trouble, and the guys sent Peaches to the house to act as my attorney. Last night was crazy, and Peaches offered to take Mina for the night so we could have a meeting."

"What did the social worker say?" Elijah slowly sat down on the stool next to Brody.

Trouble's eyes widened as Elijah reached out and took Scary's beer right out his hand—the beer that was in the process of making it to Scary's mouth. Everyone gasped, but it seemed Elijah and Brody were oblivious. Scary's only response was a grunt as he got another and then leaned back against the counter well out of reach of Elijah.

Interesting, Trouble thought and waited for Brody to answer.

"That it was a false report and agreed with Peaches about keeping a record of anything weird that happens. Peaches said anything else happens, she'd go forward with a petition for a restraining order."

"I don't want all this bullshit."

"We know that, Trouble. We just have to figure out how to get them to leave you alone." Brody hugged him tightly.

"I've met the Carvers a time or two, I always got a bad feeling about them." Elijah finished off the beer and set the bottle on the bar.

"They're miserable bastards, every last one of them."

"Scary said his crew wouldn't mind going back to jail," Lucky said from the couch.

"I think we should avoid jail time."

"He's ruining our fun," Zerk pouted.

"I'd rather not visit you in jail, and we're not officially married so no conjugal visits, I'm not giving up the one thing you do extremely well," Landon added.

"Nice to know you're only with me for my body."

"A big sexy—"

"And we're not letting this conversation devolve to sex talk, some of us aren't getting the D on the regular."

The clear pout in Lucky's voice caused them to laugh except Elijah who went bright red.

"Fine, we'll wait until we get home where it's safe for me to scream."

"And it would be gladly fucking appreciated."

"Gentlemen," Elijah muttered, and everyone snorted.

"He sounds so prim and cultured…don't you just want to get him dirty?" Lucky screamed ouch. "My dreads are fucking attached, Priest."

"Then quit being an ass."

Priest and Lucky continued to argue, but they ignored them as usual. Those two seemed to exist in their own world most of the time.

"As I was saying, we need to resolve this in a manner which shows we are the better people in the situation."

"How the fuck are we going to do that? We're not exactly allowed at your fancy country club."

"Please don't be offended, Trouble, but your family seems to believe you're inferior to them. Why do they—"

"The simple answer, they hate me. They don't give a fuck about anything but making me miserable. They don't usually start off with threats. First, they offer a payoff to the guy to leave me alone. The guys normally take it. This is the only time I know they threatened first."

Money was normally as far as they needed to go. A piece of paper was worth more than him. They'd never even offered all that much.

"You've been together longer than you were with the others. Also there's Mina. It's a small town, and people love to gossip."

"A little too much. So jail time is off the table, what are our other options?"

"We have a statement taken from Brody's boss Stan who was there when Mrs. Carver came in. Strength wise it isn't much. We have the anonymous call that came in not long after the threat." Landon paused to take the last swallow of his beer. "If Mrs. Carver was smart and I believe she is, she didn't give any identifying information. Which leaves us in a bind. All we can do is make sure we keep an eye out. Brody and Mina go nowhere alone."

"I'm not going to put everyone out."

"You'll do as we fucking say. Also, you and Princess will move into Twirled House. You don't have a choice so don't even fucking try to talk your way out of it."

"Don't speak to him like that." Elijah pointed at Scary.

"I've got a hundred on Elijah." Lucky cackled.

"I'll put you the fuck over—"

Landon was beside the bar in seconds. "Everyone calm down, no need to resort to foreplay."

Elijah turned redder than before, and Scary snarled, everyone else lost their shit and started laughing.

"You all are crazy," Elijah squeaked.

"Welcome to Twirled." Landon shook his head and went back to Zerk.

He spun on his stool and leaned forward a bit to twine his arms around Brody's waist. Setting his forehead on Brody's shoulder, he drew Brody's warmth and scent into himself and tried to calm the racing of his heart. Brody's hands stroked along his forearms.

"We'll be okay, and once this is over, it will just be a fucked up memory."

"I hope you're right."

"Everyone 's crashing here as usual. Y'all know where blankets and pillows are. No fucking in my house."

Landon and Zerk whined, causing everyone to snicker.

"I'm going home. I expect a daily check in, no excuses."

He glanced up for a second to watch as Elijah slipped off the barstool and stood to smooth his suit. He returned his head to Brody's shoulder.

"Deal, I'll call after work tomorrow," Brody answered.

"Everyone have a wonderful evening and try to stay out of jail."

Elijah's footsteps faded. He just wanted to curl up with Brody. He was so damn tired, and he wanted his life back before his family tried to fuck it up again. Everyone started talking around him, but he didn't pay attention. They didn't have any real plan. Wait and see wasn't working for him. There seemed to be no other options.

Unless they could prove what his mother did, they couldn't do anything.

It was going to be hell before it was all over. He just hoped he still had Brody and Mina when it ended.

# 15 THE CRAZY IS STRONG WITH THIS ONE

Brody was tired of being on edge on the damn time; waiting for the Carvers to make their next move. Since Scary had more control of his schedule, the huge man appointed himself Mina's bodyguard. Scary picked her up after school. She was spending more time at the Brawler House. So, there was a new set of honorary Uncles. He didn't exactly know how he felt about his baby spending time with a group of rough bouncers.

Mina adored Tank and Scary, and there was a guy named Bulletproof, Bull for short, and a man named Crave. Trouble assured him they were good men. Mina apparently had her own security team.

Speaking of security team, he smiled at his daughter strolled through the automatic doors. A huge, blond with an impish smile that looked weird on someone of his bulk and a scowling man with salt and pepper hair were behind her on either side. Mina looked like it was any other day in her new life.

"Hi, Daddy," Mina squealed and ran up to him.

He had to admit his perpetually happy daughter seemed even happier lately. Bull used to be a blacksmith and still did work here and there, so she was fascinated with whatever the man was working on recently. Crave was explicitly threatened not to teach Mina any limericks, drinking songs or dirty jokes.

"Now, what are you doing here?" He crouched down and wrapped his arms around her.

"Uncle Bull said we needed junk food because Crave ate it all last night."

"I'm a growing boy, man, got to keep up my manly physique."

"Any more manly and people are gonna start asking when you're due."

"Princess and I ain't getting you anything, old man, grumps don't get—"

"No bad words," Mina admonished.

It seemed weird Mina pointing at Crave, and he dropped his head like a kid getting in trouble. He straightened as Mina was swung up to sit on Crave's shoulder. The man took off with Crave and Mina carrying on a constant conversation about junk food and cartoons.

"Thanks for letting her hang out, Crave needs someone on his level. I'm Bull."

"Figured, I'm Brody."

"That man is eating me out of house and fucking home."

He shot Bull a confused look.

"I run the unofficial Brawlers Halfway House. I do one fucking favor, and I'm fucked for life."

"Incoming," Crave called out in a maniacal tone from one of the aisles.

"Fuck, I better make sure he doesn't tear the store down."

He laughed as Bull ambled away muttering about idiots.

"Is it just me or do you have a lot of gorgeous men hanging out recently?" Stan's voice came from behind him, and he looked over his shoulder.

"Mina acquired more Uncles."

"I see that. Watch out for Crave, that man isn't all there. Don't get me wrong, he's completely harmless, he just has very poor impulse control. Never dare him to do anything."

"I'm frightened to ask."

"You should be. I'm heading out to have lunch with Garnet."

"When's he leaving?" Garnet was an ironworker and was sent all over the country for work.

"Right after lunch. He loves his job, and I don't want to complain, but regular work close to home would be nice."

"I'm sure. I don't know what I would do if I didn't see Trouble every day."

"If you need anything just call, but I better head out."

"Okay, have a good lunch."

"If I'm a few minutes later or an hour getting back, don't worry."

He shook his head as he was left alone up front. He occasionally heard Crave and Mina' laughter and Bull's growling. The automatic doors opened, and a chime went off. He looked up from what he was doing with a smile.

When he saw the elegant woman walking toward him, all friendliness fled.

"Mrs. Carver." He was surprised by the coldness of his voice. No matter if he felt it or not, he was nice.

"I warned you, Mr. Vaughn, but I have a deal for you."

She reached into her stylish purse that probably cost more than he paid in rent for months, maybe a year. He walked out to stand in front of her. She extracted and envelope handing it to him.

"I believe it's fair compensation."

Her condescending tone grated on his nerves.

"My son with all his eccentricities and faults, he is a rather handsome man, but handsome doesn't make up for his stupidity. Unfortunately, James' only redeeming quality is probably his skills—"

"I don't believe in being rude, Mrs. Carver, but *Trouble*—" He stressed the name. "—is a wonderful man. He's an amazing parent to Mina."

She cleared her throat and tucked her purse under her arm. "Aren't even the least bit curious?"

"Yeah, aren't you curious as to what she thinks Trouble's worth?" Crave's voice drew his attention.

He turned to find Crave standing there with tons of chips, candy and countless other things in his arms, Mina hung over his shoulder like a little monkey. Her elbows braced against his massive chest, and her chin rested in her hands. He smiled at her completely contented look as if everything was perfect in her world.

"If you're not, I sure as hell am." Bull stepped up and took the envelope.

"This is a private—"

"Ain't shit—"

"Bad words, Uncle Bull."

"Sorry, Princess." Bull gave Mina an adoring smile, then it fell when he turned back to Mrs. Carver. "As I was saying, ain't nothing private in public."

He stood back and watched Bull carefully open the simple, white envelope. Bull's face remained impassive as he pulled out a check. The sudden bark of laughter was unexpected.

"Wow, I hope you paid the others more." Bull's glare was steady as he handed the slip of paper to him. The older man never took his gaze from Mrs. Carver.

Brody closed his eyes and took a deep breath, then opened them to look at what she thought her son was worth. His lungs seized up. It wasn't so much the amount she was offering for him to give up Trouble, but that she'd think he'd take it.

"I pay for what James is worth. Taking care of our disappointment—"

"Trouble isn't a disappointment. He's amazing at his job. He's a great second dad to Mina. He's proud, gorgeous and beyond sweet. I'm insulted you'd even attempt this. I don't care how many before me took it and ran, but I'm not giving up the man I love. Whether it embarrasses you or not, we're Trouble's family, not you. I think it's time for you to go."

"Yes, definitely time for you to go." Bull advanced, and Mrs. Carver retreated.

It might have been unladylike to run, but she could sure as hell power walk with the best of them.

"You enjoyed that way too much."

"I've known way too many like her. Crave, get a cart."

"On it." Crave ran off with Mina still bouncing on his shoulder.

"Those two are going to be inseparable."

"I think he might have to fight Lucky for favorite Uncle status."

"Oh no, we don't let Lucky and Crave in the same fucking room—ever. If two almost identical personalities are existing in the same space and time, it causes a catastrophic explosion of chaos and possibly signals world war three. My house barely survived their last brawl. For a skinny dude, he's goddamn vicious."

He couldn't resist laughing and then realized what Bull had done.

"Thank you."

"Don't let it get to you, yeah, she's gonna cause some damage, but fuck it. Also, don't get no ideas, I'm an asshole, and I'm cruel, so don't cast me like some fucking hero."

"Too late, um—" He pointed passed Bull's shoulder. "You might want to take care of that."

Crave and Mina were sword fighting with long loaves of bread. Both the man and Mina were giggling. He should be horrified at them corrupting his sweet daughter, but she was too happy and wasn't hurting anything.

Bull turned and growled. "Crave, put that down," the cranky man yelled and took off.

The stress of moments before was gone. He started to rip up the check but rethought the idea. Instead, he folded it and put it in his pocket to take home. He wondered if she'd offered the others more, he hoped it was more because destroying Trouble's feelings should have been worth more than paltry few thousand dollars.

He knew what the hell he wanted, Trouble and Mina, a family with them and the rest of the guys. The whole crazed Twirled and Brawler Crews who stepped up when they didn't have to do it. They needed to get Mrs. Carver to back off. The question was how to do that. He didn't want to live on constant alert, maybe it was time to bring in Elijah. Being the mayor's brother had to have its perks, right? Once work was over, he'd make the call but had a bad feeling it wouldn't be much better than having a security detail.

# 16 IS THAT ALL HE'D BEEN WORTH?

He smoothed out the edges of the wrinkled check with his fingertips. Is that all he'd been worth? Every boyfriend had taken off for the price of a pathetic shopping spree. He reached out and grabbed his empty beer bottle. He looked up and waved it to get Twitch's attention at the other end of the bar. He set the bottle on the rail as the small, feminine man nodded with a friendly smile.

Twitch strode toward him, when he stopped, he leaned forward and placed his crossed arms on the bar. "Do you really want another one, honey," Twitch asked.

"Yeah."

"Where's your DD?"

"I'm supposed to call when I'm ready to go."

Twitch lifted a perfect groomed brow. A looked that said Twitch didn't believe him.

"I promise, I have a ride. They even dropped me off."

Brody hadn't been happy about it but understood why he needed a bit of time to himself. He'd never seen evidence before. The Dear John text came in, and he never heard from them again. Why did Brody even bother with him?

"Talk," Twitch ordered.

"Nothing worth saying."

"Let me be the judge of that."

"My mother tried to pay my boyfriend off to break up with me. This is what she thought I was worth." He used the tips of his fingers to slide the check toward Twitch.

"What a bitch, you're at least worth twice that."

"Ha ha—" Trouble rolled his eyes. "—apparently, all my other boyfriends didn't think so."

"Did Brody take it?"

"No, but I don't see why he bothers with me."

"Trouble, I haven't known you long, but you're super sweet and cute in that clichéd bad boy kinda way."

"Clichéd?"

"Yeah, ya know, all muscle and good looks, rumbling in on a big ass chopper. A heartbreaker in denim and leather."

"You're so full of shit."

"Maybe." Twitch leaned in farther. "Listen, from what I hear ya got a great man and even a cute as hell little girl. So, are you gonna let this—" Twitch tapped the check with a red painted nail. "—fuck all that up?"

He dropped his forehead to the scarred bar top. Slender fingertips ruffled the hair at his nape.

"Still want that beer?"

"No, I want Brody."

"Give me your phone."

He didn't even think about it, he just reached into his back pocket and pulled out his phone. He slid it across the bar without looking up.

"Yes, this is Twitch from Brawlers—" Twitch snorted. "No, Trouble doesn't need bail. He just said he wanted you. I'm assuming you're his ride—" Twitch's fingers kept up the soothing rhythm. "I'll keep him right here. Do you want to call and I'll send him out or did you want to come in?"

He tuned out the rest of the conversation.

"Is there a fucking reason you're rubbing all over, Trouble," Crave's shouted.

Twitch shushed Crave, and he almost laughed. Crave was three times Twitch's size and slightly crazy.

"I want a fucking—"

A wet plop sound cut off Crave's demand. Trouble turned his head to find a bar towel slung over Crave's head dripping and turning his white t-shirt translucent.

"I'm not one of your little subbie boys who's gonna do everything you say."

Crave ripped the towel off his head. "I don't have subs, what the fuck are you talking about?"

"I'm kinda busy right now, and don't you have your own job to do?"

Crave clenched his jaw, and his lips pulled tight.

Twitch's running through his hair kept up the same pace. Most people saw a man like Crave, and they backed up until they reached a safe distance to run. Twitch was sweet, but sometimes he transitioned into a manic phase and became annoying as fuck.

"Thanks for taking care of him for me."

He lifted his upper body and spun on the stool at the sound of Brody's voice. He waited for anger at another man touching him.

"No problem, sweetheart." Twitch's smile was bright and innocent. "Nice to meet you in person."

"You too." Brody turned toward him. "Ready to go home, I left Mina with Lucky."

Brody twined his arms around his neck. He loosely wrapped his own around Brody's waist. He couldn't believe how much he loved Brody, but he hadn't told Brody yet. His only excuse was it terrified him that Brody didn't feel the same.

"Lucky," Crave growled the name in disgust.

"Knock it off," Twitch snapped, then went to check on the customer at the other end of the bar.

"When did you become Lucky's bestie?"

Twitch's only answer was to flip Crave off and get back to work.

He stood and pulled Brody to his side to get out of firing range. Crave didn't need an excuse to start a fight. He led Brody to the exit while listening to Crave muttering curses under his breath.

"Do those two have something going on?"

"No, Crave and Twitch barely get along, but he takes his job seriously, and he watches Twitch's back."

They stepped out into the fresh evening air, and he took a deep breath.

"Are you okay," Brody quietly asked.

"I'm sorry, I shouldn't have come here. I hope you don't think Twitch—"

"Twitch is adorable, but he was petting you like you were a puppy."

"Thanks," Trouble grunted and rolled his eyes.

144

Brody laughed. "We're a couple, but we do need time alone—to think. This was my fault. I shouldn't have showed you the check."

"No," He spun to lean back against Brody's car and pulled Brody between his spread thighs. "It's not like I didn't know she did it. You're not the first."

"I love you. No matter the amount she put on that check I wouldn't have gone anywhere."

"You love me?"

No one ever told him that or meant it if they did.

"Yes, it's silly, but I think it was the first time I saw you read to Mina. Even as uncomfortable as you looked you seemed so happy."

He took Brody's face in his hands and closed the distance between their mouths. "I love you too. Could've done this a little more romantic like and not in the parking lot of a biker bar."

"I'm quite happy with it."

He felt Brody smile against his lips, and then he kissed Brody. He didn't care about his fucked up family or how much of a disappointment he was. This was all he needed.

They broke apart at a loud symphony of wolf whistles and turned to find, Tank, Scary and the rest of the Brawler Crew standing framed in the open doors.

"No fucking in my parking lot, take that shit home. We got law abiding reps to protect—" Scary choked on a laugh.

"Boss man, couldn't even say it with a straight face," Crave yelled.

Twitch had a serene smile on his elfin face as he leaned into Tank's side.

"We gonna stand around and wait for a show or get back to fucking work," Bull asked, but before he turned, Trouble caught the man grinning.

"We're going," he spoke through his laughter.

Brody stepped away and walked around to the driver's side. In short order, they headed home.

"I'm going to call Elijah tomorrow."

"Do you think he could help?"

"Can't hurt, I mean being the mayor's brother has to have its perks."

"Okay, but I don't want him to—"

"Elijah isn't like that. He doesn't care what people think. Mayor wasn't his first career choice. He was happy being the old mayor's assistant."

"The upper crust around here isn't exactly accepting of differences."

"Elijah will be fine. I just want our lives to go back to normal."

"Whatever you think is best. I'm so tired."

Brody reached out and curved his hand around the back of his neck. Strong fingers kneaded his tight muscles, and he let his head fall back.

"Close your eyes, and I'll wake you up when we get home."

He sighed as he let his lids fall. He was tired of being stressed, and it wasn't a great situation for Brody and definitely not Princess. Okay, she thought her security detail was great, she got to hang out with her Uncles all the time, but Princess was a smart kid. It wouldn't be long before she realized something was wrong.

He felt his muscles relax as he let himself drift to sleep imagining their life together after all the bullshit was gone.

# 17 ELIJAH TO THE RESCUE

"You've been going about this all wrong," Elijah spoke in a smooth, professional tone and paced in front of them. Brody was skeptical about his brother's opinion, but was willing to listen as they gathered in Scary's basement.

"Wrong, how the fuck have we been doing it wrong?" Scary was being an asshole, bigger one than usual.

"Bodyguards, traveling in groups, great when you're waiting for a sneak attack—something violent. You need to hit them where it hurts." A terrifying smile curved Elijah's mouth. "In the country club. Public and among their peers. Appearance is everything. What you wear, who you associate with and the organizations you belong. Being considered lesser than is comparable to being a social leper."

"So, what are we doing here," Trouble asked.

"We're going to cause them the greatest of social embarrassments."

Elijah seemed way too excited, and he was slightly terrified of his brother. There was almost a maniacal gleam in the older man's eyes.

"You're talking in fucking riddles." Scary flopped back onto one of the barstools.

"We're gonna crash a party," Lucky squealed.

"How the hell did you get that from social embarrassment," Zerk asked.

Landon was stuck at work so he couldn't be in on the new meeting.

"How do you fuck up a cool kid's life," Lucky asked.

"Have the uncool kids show up at the social event of the season," Priest answered.

"You show up and pretend to rub elbows with the popular ones. Rumors fly," Elijah supplied, "Their status possibly called into question."

"So, I'm still not getting how we do that," he asked as he leaned back into Trouble and the big man instantly wrapped his arms around him.

"The Carvers are throwing a party in a week. They've invited everyone from judges, politicians, businesspeople, and yours truly. I accepted the invite."

"You're the fucking mayor, how's that going to—"

Elijah turned the sweetest smile on Scary, and the man glared.

"What the hell are you thinking?"

"I need a date to come along with me, also with Trouble and Brody."

"Aw hell Naw, I'm not gonna be some sacrificial lamb. The cops aren't exactly—"

"That's the beauty, they won't want to draw attention. Police presence and dragging one of the guests away in handcuffs—"

148

"Man, are you gonna pay my bail when your plan goes to fucking shit?"

"I can guarantee there won't be any need for bail."

"Scary, come on, help us out," Trouble asked.

"I'm not wearing a suit."

"No suits required. Hiding all those tattoos would sort of defeat the purpose. We're going to walk up in there and act like we're the Carver's best friends. They should meet their future son-in-law and in-laws."

"You're fucking twisted. For a clean-cut guy, you're vicious. I love that in a—"

Lucky flew across the room, but Scary's huge hand splayed across his chest stopped all forward movement.

"Shut up, Lucky." Scary stepped between Lucky and Elijah, "Back to your corner."

"You're always ruining my damn fun," Lucky pouted as he returned to his usual post at Priest's hip, "Can I come?"

"No, I think it'll work best with two teams. You're on babysitting duty."

"Yes, cartoon buddy." Lucky fist pumped the air. "Priest just doesn't appreciate the epic artistry."

Priest rolled his eyes.

"So, what's the complete plan," he asked.

Elijah went into planner mode and outlined what was going to happen from step one onward. He saw a new side of Elijah, and he didn't quite know how to take it. Elijah seemed quiet and timid, but professional and confident at work. His brother always had dual personalities, yet he was starting to think there was a third one—prankster and the fun-loving side that he hid beneath the three-piece suit wearing businessman.

Everyone parted ways and headed to their places or back to work. They had a plan, now to see if it worked.

♦ ♦ ♦

A week later, Brody was on the verge of puking as he sat in the back of his brother's sedan and held tight to Trouble's hand. Trouble looked handsome in his jeans and black button down shirt, the sleeves rolled up over his inked forearms. Brody dressed similarly, but he didn't look as put together.

Scary was wearing a tight black t-shirt and leather cuffs buckled around his wrists. He had on jeans that molded to thickly muscled legs. Elijah was looking casual in his button-down shirt and khakis; he'd even foregone a tie.

Everyone was silent as they thought about the parts they needed to play. He swallowed around a lump in his throat as they pulled up in front of a mansion. The place was huge and highlighted the wealth inside.

"You grew—"

"It's a cold place. You couldn't ever touch anything. Don't run. Don't talk loud. Stay in your room when we have a guest. Children should be seen and not heard. Don't embarrass us, James. It was always me while their other children were paraded around and bragged about."

"Hey, you could never be an embarrassment. Mina and I love you, remember that."

Trouble seemed nervous, and he missed Trouble's wicked smile. The way his eyes crinkled at the corners and his dimples deepened.

"Let's go be embarrassments together, I've always wanted to come out with a big party."

"Elijah, you've been out since you realized Connor Pickett had a nice ass in junior high and got your ass kicked by the junior high football team."

"Must you remind me? I ran into him a few months ago, and he was…" Elijah shuddered, "I avoided a train wreck with that one."

"Oh yeah, because Junior high relationships—"

"Don't ruin my rationalization of my terrible taste in men. It started exceptionally early and hasn't improved."

"I tried to set—"

"Oh no, you set me up with Mr. Octopus, he tried to get me into bed before—"

"Are we doing this shit or not," Scary harshly asked as he pushed open the passenger door and got out.

"Is he always so cranky?"

"Yes," him and Trouble answered together.

"Lovely." Elijah got out and closed the door.

"Are you okay, we can go home and devise another plan."

"I'm good, let's just get this over with. I hate being here."

"Just follow Elijah's lead, we can do that, right?"

Trouble nodded, and they got out, he reached for Trouble's hand and twined their fingers together. He wasn't ashamed of Trouble or the fact he loved him. And he wanted everyone to know, especially the Carvers.

They ascended the steps to stand behind Elijah and Scary. Elijah rang the bell and a lovely, middle-aged woman in a maid's uniform answered.

"James?"

"Hi, Greta."

"They didn't inform me you were invited."

"That's because they came as my guests, Mayor Vaughn."

"Mr. Vaughn, please come in. Everyone is out back in the gardens. There's an open bar, take plenty of advantage."

"Fuck, I do need a drink," Scary huffed. "Sorry, ma'am."

Everyone including him turned to Scary as if they'd never seen him before. Scary could be—polite.

"If I could I would as well, young man. Go straight back and through the formal dining room, the patio doors are open." She stepped back and motioned them through. "Good luck, Trouble."

"Thanks." Trouble smiled.

They strode through the house, and he was afraid to touch anything. Everything shone with high polish from gaudy vases to the hardwood floors. Trouble was right it, did feel cold. They quickly walked out into the late afternoon sun.

"Mr. and Mrs. Carver," Elijah's voice was louder than necessary as he waved with a flourish. "Showtime."

Elijah twined his arms around one of Scary's and stepped forward. He was surprised to see Scary not pull away.

"Mayor Vaughn, I wasn't informed you were bringing," Mrs. Carver spoke through gritted teeth, "guests."

"I thought bringing a date would be appropriate, and you should recognize your son and future son-in—"

"That pervert—"

Elijah loudly chuckled and placed his hand on the woman's forearm.

"What is going on here?" The man had silver streaked blond hair, and he looked like what he assumed Trouble would. The man was too handsome.

"Mother, Father, Elijah was nice enough—"

They instantly dismissed Trouble as if he didn't matter. He recognized the expression on Trouble's face. It was the same the man had when he'd come from the last party there.

"We don't need to hear anything from you. Did you do this on purpose?"

Although anger filled Mr. Carver's voice outwardly, he was calm and polite.

"You'll watch your fucking tone with Trouble, do you understand me," Scary growled and started to move forward.

"It is lovely to see you two as well and thank you for being so accepting of my guests." Elijah's friendliness was clearly fake, but a casual observer wouldn't know. "Now, I have a deal, it's a very simple one, apologize."

"I won't apologize to that, I should have—"

"Don't you say another fucking word, lady." He couldn't take it anymore. He tugged Trouble forward, and Elijah moved aside. "I don't care how many threats you make or how many checks you cut, I'm not leaving him. Do you know what's going to happen here today?" he asked.

They remained silent.

"We're going to drink and be happy, a lot of public displays of affection." He released Trouble's hand and hugged the man to him. "Scary here is gonna have a few too many and crash your little party. I see some of the local reporters are here. Cops and drunk bikers at your pretty party—"

"What the hell do you want to go away," Mr. Carver asked.

"Oh, it's not going to be that easy, you know why," Elijah spoke up, but didn't give them a chance to respond. "It's one thing to threaten my baby brother, but you went after my niece."

"What the hell is he talking about?" Mr. Carver turned to glare at his wife.

"Your lovely wife called social services to file a report about child endangerment. A social worker came to his home—"

"They're lying, even if I had, they are raising an innocent child."

"Inside now," Mr. Carver ordered and ushered them inside, then closed the patio doors. "Explain." He turned his attention to Brody.

"She came to my work and threatened me to stop seeing Trouble. That wasn't going to happen. My boss witnessed the exchange. Apparently, when she found out I didn't listen to her, she called to report me. Then she came to my work with a check."

"Check?"

He had a feeling the man knew nothing about what his wife was up to, and he didn't appear happy about it.

"She's bribed almost every guy I've dated. Usually, she starts off with the check, and that's that, but with Brody, she started with the threat."

"Is this true?" Mr. Carver spun toward his wife.

"I only did what was necessary. It's shameful the way he parades around town. It's a sin, and he should be ashamed to be so flagrant with his lifestyle."

"Don't say another word. James can do what he wants with his life, and I don't have to like or approve. His choices are disappointments but have nothing to do with us. You'll cease with the bribes and threats, it's one thing to go after grown men for your vendetta. You went after a child's well-being. I've taken a lot over the years, but that stops now. We'll discuss this later."

"But I only did it for the repu—"

"Stop right there. Head back outside, now," The older man's voice broached no argument.

He watched Mrs. Carver compose herself. The change so quick it made him dizzy.

"James," Trouble's father started but stopped when Trouble stepped forward.

"You and her never made it a secret y'all didn't like me."

"It wasn't that we didn't like you, James. We've never bonded. Your siblings are worse than even you, but unlike you, they'd be unable to exist without their trust funds. I won't make apologies, as you are well aware—"

"He doesn't have to be aware of anything other than you fuckers are sociopaths. What you're gonna do, is you and your psycho wife are going to leave Trouble and his family alone. If I even fucking hear about any of you anywhere near Trouble, Brody and especially Mina they won't find your fucking bodies, got it?"

Mr. Carver backed up as Scary advanced on him. He had a strong feeling the older man didn't show weakness often.

"I can guarantee it won't happen again. I'll deal with my wife in the only way she understands. Now, if it's all the same, I think we've had enough of each other's company, I'll say goodbye and have Greta—"

"We can find out own way out," Elijah politely replied.

His heart was breaking for Trouble. Trouble had his head lowered, and his shoulders slumped.

"Hey…" Scary turned and reached out to grab the back of Trouble's neck. "You look at me."

Trouble obeyed and looked up.

"Does this feel like home? Is anyone you love or loves your ass live in this place? No, they don't, so what you're gonna fucking do is go home, curl up with your family and forget all about this shit. I didn't make any idle threat. Got me?"

"Yeah, got you."

"I want pizza," Elijah announced and started through the house.

"Your brother is fucking weird," Scary muttered and followed Elijah.

"Come on, we'll go home, order pizza and curl up with our daughter, how's that sound?"

"I'd really fucking like that."

He smiled, and they made their way out of the house. Everything wasn't going to be okay, not yet, but hopefully soon. They were all quiet for the ride back to town. He curled up against Trouble and stroked the man's stomach and chest. Trouble calmed better when he was touched, and he didn't have any problem with that. They just needed to get back to normal, the way it was before the Carvers almost ruined everything.

# 18 TROUBLE, ARE YOU GOING TO BE MY PAPA?

It was another night at Brody's place. With the threat gone, he hadn't figured out how to keep Brody with him at his place. He relaxed on the couch with a sleepy Mina on his chest as they watched one of her favorite movies. Brody would be home anytime, so he was trying to keep Mina awake. The man liked to be able to tell his daughter good night and since it was Friday night she didn't have to be up early.

"Trouble?"

Mina called his name, and he turned as she placed her cute pointed chin on his chest staring at him with eyes exactly like Brody.

"What, honey," he asked as he pushed her curls from her face.

"Are you going to be my Papa? I asked Lucky, but he said I had to ask you."

"Did you talk to your Daddy about it?"

"No, but you do all the stuff Daddy does. You take me to school. Pick me up. Read me bedtime stories. I spend the night at your house. I like it better there."

Her soft confession made him smile.

Brody called Mina their daughter a week ago, after the confrontation with his parents. They hadn't talked about it since, or much of anything. It seemed Brody was keeping it light so as not to freak him out. He hadn't been helping matters either, but he'd thought about it and he wanted them to move in with him.

"I'd like to be." He didn't see a reason to lie to her. "I love you and your Daddy very much. You're going to have to ask your Daddy his feelings though. I can't answer for him."

"Daddy, can Trouble be my Papa?" Mina lifted her head as she asked.

Trouble was a bit shocked since he hadn't heard Brody come home. He tilted his head back to watch Brody walk around the couch. What would Brody's answer be, he was terrified that Brody might say no. Well, not no, but let Mina down easy.

"What did he have to say," Brody asked as he knelt on the floor in front of the couch.

"He said he'd like to be."

"Then I guess you can start calling him Papa."

She squealed and threw her arms around both their necks. She tried to squeeze the light out of them.

"It's past your bedtime. What are you still doing up?"

"I wanted to say good night. I already had my bath, I brushed my teeth, see." She smiled wide. "And Papa brushed my hair."

He knew Lucky did a better job and he could do all these different braids and shit. He'd have to ask Lucky to show him.

"Then you're all ready for bed. Come on, I'll get you settled. Tell your Papa good night."

He almost cried as two chubby arms wrapped around his neck and he sat up. "Night, Papa. You gonna spend the night?"

"Yes, I'll be here when you wake up."

She seemed satisfied and jumped up to head for her room.

"Let me get her tucked in, I'll change and be right back."

"I'll be here."

Brody kissed him and then pushed to his feet. He stood up to head for Brody's bedroom, he closed the door and stripped. He slid between the sheets and laid back to wait for Brody. The bedroom door opened, and Brody stepped through, closing it behind him.

"I figured you'd be in bed already."

Brody moved toward the bed, toed off his shoes and started to remove his clothes.

"Move in with me?" Trouble barely kept himself from asking this past week.

"Into Twirled House," Brody asked as he removed all his clothes and crawled into the bed curling up to his side.

"Not really, there's a guest house out back, it isn't huge, and there's only a tiny kitchen, but it's about the same size as this place. I already talked to the guys."

"How do they feel about a kid in their space?"

"Lucky's already working on the guest house and decorating her room. If you don't want to, we can keep everything as it is."

"When do I move in," Brody asked as Brody lifted to straddle his hips.

"Tomorrow?"

"It's month to month here, I'll give my notice tomorrow that I'll be out by the end of the month."

"That works. Now, it's been a whole twenty-four hours since I've had any loving." He pouted.

"I'm such a terrible boyfriend."

"Completely, I don't see how I keep you around." He grinned as he palmed Brody's hips.

Brody lifted onto his knees and moved down his body. He watched as Brody tugged the sheet down to expose Trouble's hardening cock. Brody licked up the length of his cock from balls to pierced head. His hips jerked off the mattress, and he combed his fingers through Brody's hair, drawing his nails over Brody's scalp. He was so close to the edge, but with Brody, his control was shit.

He gripped Brody's biceps and pulled him up to his body until Brody's mouth hovered above his. Rubbing his hands down Brody's back to his ass he guided them to their cocks slid together.

"Ya gonna get yourself ready for me," he asked he reached under the pillow for the lube and condom he'd left there earlier.

Brody traced his lips with the tip of his tongue and then sucked at them as Brody took the bottle, then straightened. Brody quickly slicked his fingers and reached behind him.

"Fuck, I love watching you." He touched every inch of Brody he could reach. Savoring his softness, kneading the slight swell of his stomach and Brody arched, moaning above him. He'd never seen anyone so fucking beautiful.

Brody's mouth fell open, and his eyes fluttered closed, his lover's body trembled as Brody moved his hips back and forth. Brody's pale skin flushed. He wrapped his hand around both of their hard dicks and jacked them in a tight fist. Slow and easy. His body heated and sweat beaded on his brow. His balls ached and his cock pulsed, he used his thumb to spread the drops of pre-come, using it to ease the stroke of his hand.

"Need you," Brody whimpered.

"Lift up, baby," he ordered and placed one hand on Brody's ass, flexing his arm to move Brody up. He released their cocks and circled the base of his dick. "You're in control."

Brody jerked his head in a quick nod as he reached back to part his cheeks and start to lower himself. He held his breath at the slight resistance before Brody's hole relaxed and let him in.

They groaned in unison as he sunk deep. The squeeze got him every fucking time. So tight and perfect, made just for him. Brody's breathing was ragged, and his teeth were deep in the curve of his bottom lip. His man's rounded ass met his thighs, and they stayed that way until Brody adjusted to the thickness.

"Ride me," he growled.

Brody leaned forward to slam his mouth onto his. The kiss was all tongue and teeth, rough and desperate as Brody started to bounce his hips up and down. He dug his heels into the bed and thrust upward to meet Brody's downward stroke. The sounds of sex filled the room, and the scent of clean sweat and Brody's skin filled his nostrils.

Every muscle in his body strained, contracting and relaxing. His ass flexed with each brutal lift of his hips. He grabbed Brody's hip with his left hand and slid the other along the crease of his ass. His middle and index finger bracketed his dick, he massaged the stretched rim. Brody's forehead fell to his chest and his back arched.

"You fucking like this," he growled as he lifted his head to bite down on Brody's shoulder. He needed more, he flipped Brody onto his back and placed his arms under Brody's knees as he moved faster and harder.

Brody screamed his name. He cut it off with his mouth. He rode Brody hard as he felt Brody's fist working a frantic rhythm against his stomach.

"Do it, cum on my dick, fucking—"

Teeth sank into his chest as wet heat spread between them. Brody whimpered around the flesh pinched hard between his teeth. The pain drove him on until he couldn't hold out, his thrusts became erratic as his balls drew up to his body and came. He threw back his head but clenched his teeth to stay quiet.

His muscles shook as he released Brody's legs and collapsed on top of him. His softening cock slipping from the tight grip of Brody's hole. He moaned at the loss as he placed kisses across Brody's collarbones. Trouble tasted the tang of his sweat.

"Love you," Brody whispered.

Brody's fingers massaged up and down his back in a soothing pattern.

"Love you too, thank you for not giving up on me."

"I'd never do that."

"I know. Maybe one day you'll want to marry me?"

"Is that you asking or just asking my opinion on marriage?"

"Maybe a bit of both."

"Yes then, but only if I get a cool ring like Landon's."

"Maybe we can work something out."

He laughed as Brody pushed at his shoulders and he rolled to his back. Brody got up and reached for the pajama bottoms Trouble had taken off.

"I need a shower and bed. Our daughter gets up way too early."

"Ours, I like the sound of that."

He contentedly whispered as he listened to the door open and close. The air cool against his sweaty skin as he thought about all the shit that changed in the past year. He didn't know what he did right, but he wasn't going to complain. He was going to make sure Brody never regretted saying yes.

# EPILOGUE: INKED BANDS AND HAPPILY EVER AFTER

*Eight Months Later...*

He sat on Trouble's lap as the man held a conversation with the whole crew including Gib and Peaches. He stroked the thick band of black around his ring finger. Trouble had tattooed it there a few months before, and Zerk added a matching one to Trouble's finger. It was becoming a tradition carried over from Gib and Peaches, same with the tattoos on anniversaries.

Mina was off with Lily for some music festival and a sleepover. That had been an experience, meeting the Trenton family. He'd thought Lucky was weird, but he was almost normal in comparison. Which was terrifying. Although the woman loved Mina and got as much honorary grandma time as she could.

Scary growled, and everyone's attention went to the door to find Elijah standing nervously just inside. He didn't know what Scary had against Elijah, but it was starting to piss him off.

"Elijah, you came." He shook off Trouble's hands with a laugh as he headed toward his brother.

"I can't stay long, where's Mina?"

"Princess," the whole crew corrected, and he rolled his eyes.

"She's at a music festival with Lily and Damon."

"She has quite the social life."

"Don't start pouting." Elijah still had some issues with sharing, but it was kind of understandable. She had a schedule of sleepovers, music festivals, camping trips and a few tattoo conventions.

"I'm not, can you pencil me in for a weekend, maybe dinner?"

"Yeah, why don't you come get her next Saturday?"

"Deal, I—" Elijah glanced passed his shoulder then away quickly. "I really should get going. "

"Stay, we're all just hanging out, you're welcome."

"No, I'm not."

There was another one of those quick peeks then Elijah couldn't get out of the door fast enough. Elijah was getting steadily weirder over the last few months. That was the first time in months he'd seen him. He didn't mind if they came to visit him, but wouldn't come to their place. Shaking his head, he went back to Trouble, and the man patted his lap.

"I can get my own seat."

"Yeah, you could, but that's too fucking far away. Come on, you know you wanna."

He snorted and retook his seat on Trouble's lap.

"Elijah okay, he left quick," Peaches asked.

"Yeah, I guess he had something to do."

He leaned back against Trouble's chest and listened to the conversations going on around him. A lot changed since he moved in with Trouble. He couldn't say everything was perfect, but it damn near was. He now had a huge family, a partner and his daughter was happy and healthy.

Saying no to Trouble all those times delayed the inevitable. This was where he was meant to be, now if he could just figure out what was going on with Elijah. It was the only dark spot. He wanted Elijah to feel like he belonged with the Twirled Crew, his big brother needed them just as much as he did. And he wasn't going to take it for granted—family and love were everything.

## THE END

# ABOUT THE AUTHOR

By day, J.M. is an introverted cook hiding out in her kitchen in the middle of nowhere Ohio, by night and any free time she may have, she is a writer of mainly LGBTQ Fiction and Erotica. Although. she's equal opportunity when it comes to telling a story, she'll even write a bit of straight erotic romance when the mood strikes.

She has been writing for years in old notebooks. At the age of eight, she wrote the worst poem in the history of poetry, but it sparked her love for writing. She reads too much and loves to get lost in other worlds and her favorite stories have to include laughter and having the reader doing at least one double take. Thirty-something, forever restless she uses her stories to ground herself, and find her place of peace.

WHERE TO FIND J.M.
www.jmdabneyauthor.com

# AVAILABLE NOW

### SCARY
Twirled World Ink 3

Welcome to Twirled World Ink where the crazies run the asylum.

Gene Sheridan earned the appropriate nickname when Legend Gib Phelps employed him at Twirled World Ink—Scary. No one made it out of his old neighborhood without scars both mental and physical. At one time, Scary thought he had a chance—that is until his ex found slumming with someone like him wasn't worth his trust fund. No-strings hookups became his go-to when he needed to relieve some tension. Co-owning a bar called Brawlers with his best friend, Tank, made it easy to find a body to use for the night. If not happy, he was content with his life, but contentment was starting to seem like a terrible thing.

Elijah Vaughn worried about everything. His life was put on hold at eighteen when his mostly-absent parents died on one of their many adventures, leaving him to raise his six-year-old brother, Brody. He'd never had anything or anyone that was just his. When Brody met a tattoo artist named Trouble, Elijah hadn't realized how much it would change his life. He met a massive man named Scary, and he was terrified how the man made him feel.

Tank Davis lost his voice the night he was attacked and had this throat slit ear-to-ear. Silent and intimidating, he scared off more men than he drew. Scary and he made a life for themselves in a small town in Georgia. Most nights everyone could find him working security at the door. Scary called in a favor and Tank met the one man he couldn't resist, proper and upstanding Elijah Vaughn.

Can one man accept there's not one perfect man for him, but two damaged souls who need him to be whole?

✦ ✦ ✦

## 1 ALL HAIL THE BASTARD

The music from inside Twirled World Ink vibrated the door as Gene "Scary" Sheridan pulled it open and walked inside. He shouldered off his leather jacket as he strode across the room to make his way behind the reception desk. Scary threw the jacket over the back of the chair and sat down picking up the stack of messages. He flipped through them not paying much attention. Shop manager or not, he didn't fuck with the paperwork.

When he'd hired on to the Twirled World Crew he damn sure didn't anticipate becoming the keeper of the rest of the crazies who worked there. When he heard the breakroom door creak open, he jerked his head around.

"Scary, when did you sneak in?" Trouble, artist and piercer, popped out of the door.

"Just now, glad I wasn't a fucking customer."

"The chime just went off, so relax."

That was Trouble, he was the most laid back member of the crew especially since he hooked up with his boyfriend, Brody. Trouble seemed to be on the road to permanent commitment just like the only other attached artist, Berzerker.

Scary looked up as the chime went off, he groaned as Mayor Elijah Vaughn, Brody's brother, breezed in. His perfectly tailored suit highlighted the trim lines of his body. All dark hair and clear blue eyes, wholesome and shit, *All American Apple Pie.*

"Mr. Sheridan," Elijah's smooth Southern accent and bright smile brightened the room—how fucking clichéd was that?

"Scary," he corrected a bit more briskly than he intended, but it wasn't like his nickname didn't fit him. He was a fucking beast, and he had no problem playing it up mainly to keep men like Elijah away from him. Because what he wanted to do to that slim body was probably illegal in most states, at the very least it would send the proper politician running in the opposite direction. "What can I do for you, Mr. Mayor?"

"Please, call me Elijah, we go through this every time, Mr.—Scary."

"What can I do for you?" he enunciated and knew he was a major dick, but at the moment, he didn't care. People didn't call him a bastard for nothing.

"Yes, well, I was just walking by and thought I'd say hello."

He remained silent and stared the man down. Elijah shifted nervously from one foot to the other and shoved his hands deep into the pockets of his tailored slacks. What the fuck would he do with a perfectly primped man in tailored suits? No man like that wanted to get dirty with a fucker like him.

"I better get going. I have a lunch engagement. It was nice to see you again…Scary, have a good day, Trouble."

"You too, Elijah. Hey, you need to come to dinner. Brody and I were talking it's been awhile since you've seen your niece."

"That would be wonderful. Tell Brody to call me. Keeping track of his and Mina's schedules is hard. I don't want to be—" Elijah fell into silence and stared down at the spotless, shined toes of his wingtip dress shoes.

"You're never a bother, Elijah. You can come by Twirled House anytime."

"Thank you, Trouble. Good day."

Elijah did a perfect turn on his toes and strode quickly to the exit, within seconds he was through the shop door and out of view of the large picture windows.

"Do you always have to be a dick to him?"

"What the fuck are you talking about?"

He knew what Trouble accused him of, and he didn't know why he shrugged it off as if he didn't know. Scary had his reasons, and they weren't Trouble or anyone else's business.

"You make him feel like something disgusting you stepped in. He's a good guy. A bit shy and lonely, but he's nice to me, to everyone since Brody and me got together. No better than attitude."

"I don't care what his attitude is. I got shit to do and don't you have better things to do than getting into shit that ain't your business?"

"Yeah, I do."

He barely paid attention to Trouble leaving him alone in the main room as he exited to the employee's only section.

He was a fucking asshole. They'd known it for years, so he didn't see why Trouble made a big deal out of it. He didn't have time for pretty boys in the mood to slum. When he wanted a fuck, he found a man like him who knew the score and didn't have dreams of some fabled happily ever after in their damn eyes.

The phone rang, and he picked up the receiver. "Twirled."

"What was this I heard you were rude to a customer," his boss, Gib Phelps' voice growled in his ear.

"Trouble," Scary bellowed, and a grinning pain in the ass peeked out of the employee break room and then ducked out of sight.

"Don't yell at Trouble."

"It wasn't a fucking customer, just Elijah." Scary scrubbed his hand over his shaved head and held in a growl.

"Quit being mean to Elijah. That boy ain't done shit to you."

"He ain't a boy, he's a grown ass man who can take care of himself."

Okay, Elijah being self-sufficient pulled at the reins of possible. He guessed the man handled himself well at work, but personally he'd heard Elijah couldn't get more lost. Gib's voice jolted him out of his head, and he rolled his eyes.

"Says the bastard of Twirled."

"I'm not doing this with you, old man. Elijah's my business." Fuck, he shouldn't have said that. Scary already had too much responsibility with the Twirled Crew and his from the bar he owned. He sure has hell didn't want to add to his personal and professional workload; soothing the timid Elijah would transition into a full-time job.

"He ain't none of your business, but if you don't start being nice, I'm gonna sic Peaches on you."

Shit, to be honest, he was terrified of Peaches more than Gib. She'd worked as a public defender in Atlanta. Her connections were a hell of a lot more dangerous than his. He joked about hiding a body or two, but Peaches knew men who could make it happen.

"Don't threaten me with your wife."

"I'll do what I want. He's related to my son-in-law."

"Trouble's not your kid, and Brody's not your son-in-law."

"I adopted all you shits the day I hired y'all. Don't make me come down there."

Scary suppressed the need to laugh at the threat. It amused the hell out of him when Gib tried to play father figure with him. He was almost a foot taller and a hundred pounds heavier than Gib.

"Like I'm scared of a geriatric canvas of skin and bones."

"Peaches, Scary's being a bastard."

He grimaced and held the phone away from his ear.

Scary huffed and tipped his head back to stare at the ceiling. He didn't want to deal with Peaches. The beautiful middle-aged woman could be worse than a mama bear when she thought one of her boys was in trouble.

"Scary, are you hurting Elijah's feelings again?"

"Dammit, he's grown and able to handle his shit. He doesn't need bodyguards."

"He's a sensitive and lonely young man. You know he comes to the damn shop just to see your ugly mug."

Scary couldn't ignore the truth of Peaches' statement. The first time he met Elijah, he would've had to be blind not to notice Elijah sneaking glances at him from under the long, thick fringe of his lashes. He'd caught Elijah moving toward him when Lucky one of the Twirled Crew tried flirting. Scary couldn't be some savior to the gorgeous man.

"I'm not ugly." He wasn't handsome either. Scary knew what he looked like; he'd stared at himself enough in his forty-three years to have every scar on his harsh face memorized.

"You're not pretty, and you're over forty, you're not getting any younger."

"I do fine." And he did, it didn't matter if he didn't remember half their names or even cared too. They got each other off and wasn't that the point of fucking?

"With your left hand probably, actual human beings not so much."

"Don't be mean," he growled.

"How does it feel?"

"Peaches, you're not going to guilt me into being nice to Elijah."

"I'm done with you, Gib, he's all yours. When he acts like this, he's yours. I'm not claiming this one."

He hung up the phone without waiting for Gib to come back on the line. He didn't have time for that shit. Scary tossed the messages back on the desk, ripped his jacket off the back of the chair, and headed for the door without a word.

He'd backed his *Harley Softail* up to the curb. Twirled World's Main Street location considered prime real estate in Powers, Georgia. For small town America, it leaned toward eclectic, and he liked it there. He'd lived there over a decade, and he hadn't had the urge to run yet.

Scary grabbed his helmet and slipped it on, he didn't have any appointments that day. A long ride would clear his head before he had to be at his bar, Brawlers, for the evening shift.

Why everyone had to jump to Elijah's defense pissed him off. It wasn't his problem the man was over-sensitive. His unwanted attraction to the man aggravated his bastard tendencies. He'd learned decades before pretty boys were nothing but trouble. The one time he'd let a man passed his defenses, he'd been fucked over. Callum was all innocent, appeared so fucking loving, but the moment Scary turned his back, Callum fucked the first respectable man he could take home to the family.

Ugly, tattooed and scarred, Gene Sheridan was just a piece of trash from the wrong side of the tracks. Men like Elijah were all the same, and he didn't give a fuck how many people talked about how sweet and lonely the man was. It wasn't his fucking business. Scary wouldn't let a repeat of the past come around again. Elijah could stay on his side of the tracks and leave Scary to his own life.

His bike rumbled to life, and he rolled onto the deserted street toward the town limits. He was alright just like he was, and he wasn't going to change because some boy got his panties in a bunch. Clearing his head, he settled looser on the seat and lost himself in the warmth of the sun, the wind whipping around him and forgot his troubles for a few hours. On the road he felt at peace, he refused to let bullshit intrude and ruin it.